Don't Drink and Die

Seemingly from out of nowhere, a lively leprechaun appeared and placed a pitcher of green beer in front of Charlie Fione. The senator laughed, leaned into his mike, and, affecting an Irish brogue, said, "Happy St. Patrick's Day. And may we all be in heaven a half hour before the devil knows we're dead!" Fione graciously filled Halligan and Romero's glasses before his own.

Holly clicked her glass against Charlie's and Rickie's, then held it up as if to toast the audience, saying, "Erin go Bragh!" Shouts of approval swept through the ball-room as the panelists raised their beers to their lips.

Charlie Fione screamed first. Then rolled from his seat, grabbing at his throat, and landed, clutching his stomach, on the Persian carpet. Holly Halligan's mouth formed a perfect O, but nothing came out. On my feet, stepping on Gypsy Rose's pumps, trying to get to the head table, I watched Holly tumble to the floor, thrashing and flaying. Not a pretty picture. Rickie Romero shook his head as if in violent denial, then crashed face first into the bowl of shamrocks on the table in front of him. Modesty, who'd scampered out of the row before me, videotaped the ghastly scene while Dennis dialed 911 and my mother cried, "God help us! Someone has killed them all!"

Don't miss these other Jake O'Hara
Ghostwriter mysteries . . .

GHOSTWRITER
DEATH COMES FOR THE CRITIC

Death Never Takes a Holiday

Noreen Wald

BERKLEY PRIME CRIME, NEW YORK

To my sister, Helen Feeley Brennan,
and her husband, Thomas Patrick Brennan

This is a work of fiction. Names, characters, places, and incidents are
either the product of the author's imagination or are used fictitiously,
and any resemblance to actual persons, living or dead, business
establishments, events, or locales is entirely coincidental.

DEATH NEVER TAKES A HOLIDAY

A Berkley Prime Crime Book / published by arrangement with
the author

PRINTING HISTORY
Berkley Prime Crime edition / November 2000

The Penguin Putnam Inc. World Wide Web site address is
http://www.penguinputnam.com

ISBN: 0-425-17744-0

Berkley Prime Crime Books are published
by The Berkley Publishing Group,
a division of Penguin Putnam Inc.,
375 Hudson Street, New York, New York 10014.
The name BERKLEY PRIME CRIME and the BERKLEY PRIME CRIME
design are trademarks belonging to Penguin Putnam Inc.

PRINTED IN THE UNITED STATES OF AMERICA

10 9 8 7 6 5 4 3 2

One

"Doesn't Death get St. Patrick's Day off?" Modesty demanded. I looked up at her and grinned, marveling at her kelly-green monk's robe, its belt bedecked with fresh shamrocks. Where in God's name had she found it? She didn't smile back. "Come on, Jake, exit that computer. Now! The parade will pass us by!"

Since her arrival five minutes ago, Modesty had been complaining and pacing back and forth, from the bedroom window to my desk, as I suffered from my usual scene-of-the-crime phobia and tried to ignore her. You'd think a fellow ghost might be a tad more understanding. My current employer's plot revolved around a former chorus girl turned serial killer and he'd insisted that every decapitation be choreographed to the sound of music. Preferably Rodgers and Hammerstein's. Any murder setting sent me into writer's block, but struggling with the sixth sing-along site, I felt I might be imprisoned there for life.

Maybe I should obey Modesty's marching order. Our

panel in the Grand Ballroom of the Plaza Hotel wasn't scheduled until three, but the Greater New York Crime Writers' Conference started at one. If we wanted to see any of the parade, we should get going. I closed the file on death.

It was damn chilly in Carnegie Hill this morning. I dug into my parka's pockets looking for my gloves. March had come in like a lion and the king of beasts still roared. No sign of any lamb lurking, to lead us into spring. The air felt clean and crisp. God help all those drum majorettes, freezing their tushes off. I found my gloves and pulled my hood up. Modesty wore an Irish tweed cape, which covered her from chin to shin. But her head remained bare. And her short, tousled, pale red hair—like her belt—was intertwined with shamrocks. Those three-leaf clovers would never hold in place until we arrived at St. Patrick's. Fortunately, the wind whipping across town from the East River was at our backs.

As we passed Mr. Kim's grocery store—its outdoor fruit stand blanketed in protective plastic wrap—on the southeast corner of Ninety-second and Madison, my mother, bundled in layers of taupe and beige wool, her sand-colored bangs barely visible beneath a matching cloche, emerged. Not a smidgen of green—except for the emerald in her Irish eyes—could be found anywhere on her slim figure. Despite her heritage, Maura O'Hara wouldn't be caught dead wearing large patches of kelly green. Not even on St. Patrick's Day. She considered the color to be unlucky. No tinge of green has ever crossed our co-op's threshold. "We're beige people," Mom had once told me when we were redecorating. And she'd spread out sample paint-shade cards—ranging from eggshell to ecru—for my monochromatic consideration.

Today, she carried a taupe mesh tote filled with bagels and melons, and was chatting away with Mr. Kim. Or chatting at him. Mom seldom paused for responses. But that didn't matter; Mr. Kim appeared to be fascinated by her every word.

"How are you girls getting downtown?" Mom asked as soon as she spotted us. "You can't possibly walk. It's only thirty degrees out, you know. Thank God, it's supposed to warm up this afternoon. Of course, Fifth Avenue's closed for the parade, so the buses aren't running, a taxi's scarcer than a hen's tooth, and the subway will be packed!" She wrinkled her nose, dismissing the IND line as an option. I waited, positive Mom would provide us with a travel plan. Modesty said nothing. I guess by now she, too, knew my mother had all the answers.

But it was Mr. Kim who did the talking. "Dennis can drive Jake and Modesty down Park Avenue," he said to my mother, then turned to me. "You know that Dennis always finds a parking place." Oh yeah, I knew. I don't think Dennis Kim has parked legally since he became a hotshot entertainment attorney and started tooling around town in his cream-colored Rolls-Royce convertible. His father continued, "Then you all can walk over to the cathedral, together. Hey, no big deal, he planned to stop at the cardinal's reviewing stand, anyway, before heading over to that crime conference at the Plaza. He's bringing the car around now and he only has one other passenger."

Mr. Kim reached behind the plastic wrap and pulled out two bananas, handing one each to me and Modesty. "Eat these in the car. I'll go inside and get you some hot coffee." He scurried off as my mother nodded, approvingly. Oh, great, I thought. I'm sure Dennis will love Modesty and me turning his luxurious, pale cream leather rear seats into a diner.

Now, why would Dennis Kim, my childhood nemesis, sometime business associate, and long-term on-again/off-again crush, be attending the Greater New York Crime Writers' Conference? Dennis could forecast a blockbuster from the first line of a book proposal. Which high-profile crime writer was he representing? And how had he managed to be included among all the Catholic hierarchy on the steps of St. Patrick's Cathedral? Mom had won two of those hard-to-get spots while playing roulette during a Las Vegas Night at St. Thomas More's. How had Dennis come by his? Maybe his new client was the cardinal? Or the mayor? Either one of them might have a murder-mystery plot just waiting to be turned into a best-seller.

"Listen, Mrs. O'Hara, your lucky number won these passes, are you sure you don't want to go to the parade?" Modesty asked my mother for about the tenth time.

"No, to tell you the truth, I overdosed on 'Danny Boy' decades ago." My mother laughed. "All those high-school fife-and-drum corps have taken their toll. I'm going to have a bagel, some fruit, and a nice, hot cup of tea. Maybe I'll catch the beginning on TV, then I have an appointment for a blow-dry. You two have a good time, but don't be late for the conference kickoff. Holly Halligan and Senator Fione! Two of my all-time favorites!! I can't wait. Gypsy Rose and I will meet you at the Plaza. Around noon. We'll grab a bite to eat. Her parapsychology panel is scheduled right after yours. Then we all can have a St. Patrick's Day drink in the Palm Court." Satisfied that we had Dennis to transport us, Mom headed home.

"Even I know who Charlie Fione is," the apolitical

Modesty said. "That old stuffed turkey of a senator who's been in office since before I was born, but who the hell is Holly Halligan?"

"So, would you ladies like to ride with the top down?" Dennis Kim's chariot had arrived. And, as always, the glint in his gold-flecked eyes sent steam heat straight down to my toes.

His passenger—and client—turned out to be more impressive than either the cardinal or the mayor. And, boy, would Mom be sorry that she'd decided to pass on the parade. After Modesty and I had settled into the backseat, precariously balancing our coffee cups, Dennis drove straight across Ninety-second Street, went less than a half block north on Madison, and double-parked in front of the Hotel Wales. Holly Halligan, former MGM superstar and my mother's childhood idol, swept out of the lobby and swooped into our lives.

Ms. Halligan, sensational at seventy-four—or considerably older, if you believed the *National Enquirer*'s source—wore a ski suit. Bold blue with crisp white stripes on the legs and sleeves. Formfitting. Flattering her slim and, seemingly, firm figure. Her silver hair was tucked under a politically incorrect but totally smashing blue fox hat. Huge royal-blue sunglasses covered her eyes. Mom had told me Holly Halligan's bright blue eyes were once as much admired and as famous as Elizabeth Taylor's violet ones.

"Call me Holly!" Her star quality filled the front passenger seat. "Say, Jake, you look like Annie Hall. And wasn't Diane too divine in the role?" Giving Modesty and me a warm smile, Holly placed a Virginia Slim in a royal-blue cigarette holder and flicked a matching lighter, took a deep puff, then said to Dennis, "Does this car have a bar? I crave a bit of bourbon, but anything will suffice."

Enlisted as bartender, I poured a shot of Jack Daniel's for Holly from the tiny built-in cabinet, which contained only a handful of those miniatures that you see on airplanes, while Dennis gave Holly's first murder mystery a rave review. Modesty juggled the two coffee cups and, sotto voce, whispered, "Who is this broad?"

The ex–movie star and current best-selling author had excellent hearing. "I'm the broad who exposed Louie B. Mayer. My only regret is that I waited over a half century to write *Murder at MGM*." Holly took off her sunglasses and her bright, blue eyes stared into Modesty's paler ones. "Haven't you read it or, at least, read about it? The *Times* said I killed like an old pro."

Modesty, considered by many of our fellow ghost-writers to be a misogynist—I'm about the only woman she tolerates—snarled, "I write; I don't read." Churning out anonymous murder-mysteries-for-hire and mired in almost two thousand pages of her own gothic novel-in-progress, this was her standard—if somewhat startling—reply to any and all questions dealing with current literature. And, often, current events.

Holly remained undaunted. "My mystery stars Mayer as a multiple murderer."

I reached across the front seat, handing Holly her straight whiskey. She put her glasses back on and downed it in one gulp.

"Of course, the book is fiction," Dennis said, like the lawyer he was.

"Anyone who's anyone on the coast knows it's true," Holly countered. "Well, not the killings, of course. Actually, most of the studio's stars wanted to murder Mayer. And it's the hottest book on Amazon's list. I'm famous all over again. People are pestering me for my autograph. There's even a Holly Halligan Skis retrospective at the Museum of Modern Art's theater. I'm a household name among New Yorkers!" She jerked her thumb, like a hitchhiker, at Modesty. "Except for her."

"Did you say skis?" Modesty sounded even more miserable than usual.

Dennis caught my eye in the rearview mirror and winked. "Modesty, I'd just bet that Maura O'Hara's daughter could fill you in on Holly Halligan's Hollywood heyday."

I knew a cue when I heard it. "Holly's one of Mom's five favorite film stars. In the late forties and early fifties, Esther Williams swam her way into silver-screen stardom, but Holly, who, as Mom has pointed out, could also act, skied her way through a series of MGM musicals. All box-office triumphs. Mom still watches her *Swedish Sunrise* video at least once a week."

"Thank your mother for her loyalty. So many fans forget. *Swedish Sunset* is my favorite movie, too. Ingrid Bergman helped me with the accent," Holly said, doing a pretty good Ilsa Lund.

Modesty stared at Holly. "You know, you *do* look familiar."

Holly smiled and handed me her paper cup for a refill. "Well, perhaps, you've seen some of my long-ago hits on AMC. From the glory days when I was young." Holly sighed and reached for her fresh drink.

"I didn't know you ever were young." Modesty shook her head from side to side. "I'm talking about now. How you look now. I've seen you somewhere . . . maybe . . . on tel—"

Dennis said, "Holly's the national spokesperson for Ashes Away. She does all their TV commercials."

"What the hell is that?" Modesty asked.

Holly went into her spiel. "It's a total-concept cremation service: book now; later your ashes will embark on a short final voyage, where your loved ones can scatter you to the wind. If you have no family, the company will arrange to have a designated flinger aboard at a small additional cost."

"That's an outrageous way to earn a living!" Modesty said.

"Yes, isn't it! Cheers!" Holly drained her cup. "But the pay is wonderful and I do believe in the product. My own arrangements are all made. A cruise through the fjords. In a ship shaped like a ski. I've asked Jean-Claude Killy to provide my last fling. Furthermore, if June Allyson can hawk Depends, Holly Halligan can promote Ashes Away."

Modesty moaned as Dennis pulled into a no-parking zone between Park and Madison on Fiftieth Street. "Okay, ladies, we've arrived. Just a block and a half away from St. Pat's. Let's go to the parade."

But as we buttoned up our overcoats, Holly had the last word. "I urge you all to plan ahead. Make your reservations now! Cremation cruises are the wave of the twenty-first century."

TWO

A light snow fell, caressing the bare branches of the trees scattered along Fiftieth Street. A pretty, late-winter scene, but potentially dangerous. The marchers would have to watch their steps on the slick ground.

The mournful tones of "The Irish Soldier Boy," no doubt performed by one of Mom's dreaded high-school bands, wafted over from Fifth Avenue and accompanied our little troop as we trudged west to St. Pat's.

Holly sang along to the music. A clear, on-key, but equally sorrowful-sounding soprano. As a child and a teenager, that song always had reduced me to tears. Even as an adult, I'd found it moving. Today, its sad words irritated me. Jesus, could I be turning into my mother?

"I get seasick, you know." Modesty's strident voice disturbed my reverie.

"What?" I asked as Holly started the third stanza. To my further annoyance, Dennis's deep baritone had joined in on the chorus.

"Why would I want my soul to sail off into the sunset?" Modesty grumbled. "This ghost's going to a cemetery. I want to be buried in terra firma. Tomorrow morning, I'm adding a codicil to my will—making sure that I'm planted, not flung!"

Since Modesty never joked, I knew she must be dead serious.

Dennis, obviously capable of eavesdropping while singing, asked her, "Do you need a lawyer?"

Modesty scowled at him as the band segued into an upbeat, trumpet-heavy rendition of "When Irish Eyes Are Smiling."

The doormen at the Palace Hotel, dressed in regalia better suited for an operetta than the sidewalks of New York, were attempting to cope with the masses. Visitors from the outer boroughs, Long Island, and New Jersey, almost like aliens from another planet compared with the hotel's usual clientele, literally, were storming the Palace's gates, beer cans in hand, and laughing at the uniform of the day.

By the time we forged across Madison, Fiftieth Street had turned into a sea of green. Hordes of people, all jockeying for positions closer to the line of march, made it difficult to navigate. I could see that the police barricades on Fifth Avenue, separating the spectators from the marchers, seemed ready to collapse as the cops on horseback barked orders while attempting to keep the crowd at bay. "When Irish Eyes Are Smiling" got louder and louder.

At the side door of St. Patrick's, closest to Madison Avenue, Dennis took Holly Halligan's hand. "This is where we leave you, ladies. I'll bet we beat you to the cathedral steps," he said to Modesty and me, and started toward the door.

Holly sang, " 'Sure, it's like a morn in spring'!"

"Where are you going?" I asked him.

" 'In the lilt of Irish laughter.' " Holly belted out the line.

"I always approach the reviewing area this way." Dennis smiled. God, those gold-flecked eyes were beautiful. "Cut through the church, go out the center front door, and—Erin Go Bragh—there I am on the steps, right next to the cardinal!"

" 'You can hear the angels sing'!" Holly hit the high notes.

"You're a gate-crasher!" I screamed over the blaring band, outshouting Holly's strong soprano.

Dennis nodded. "Have been for years." He sounded so bloody proud of himself. "I'm a fixture now. Everyone assumes I'm on the list. All the bishops are my buddies. Hurry up, I want you to witness how warmly His Eminence greets me."

Modesty said, "Dennis Kim, where are your ethics? You deserve to be disbarred! Shakespeare had it right: 'First, we kill all the lawyers'!"

"Relax, Modesty," Dennis said. "This year, I actually received an invitation. The cardinal's putting together a book proposal on the history of the Catholic Church in New York and he wants me to represent him. But it's more fun to sneak in this way. Last one to land on the steps buys the first drink at the Plaza." He entered the cathedral. Holly Halligan, still singing, followed him.

Modesty and I arrived at the front steps—after a brief but very unpleasant encounter with a mounted policeman who'd thought we were trying to push our way to the front lines and decided to make an example out of us—just in time to see Dennis Kim kiss the cardinal's ring. I prayed there was a hell.

Snowflakes swirled as the Fighting 69th marched by.

The famous Irish regiment's heroic war story had been made into a movie that had been my late father's favorite. Mom and I still rented it every couple of years. Then, while the County of Cork approached, Dennis introduced Modesty and me to the cardinal. Thrilled, as only a former Catholic convent-school girl could be, I nervously bent to kiss the archbishop of New York's ring. Though I sensed that Dennis was smirking behind me, I didn't care. Even the music sounded better. Then Modesty, greeting the cardinal, smiled. And, suddenly, I didn't even feel the cold.

Wow, wouldn't Maura O'Hara have gotten a kick out of all this? Maybe next year, Dennis could sneak Mom in with him. Or, if the cardinal's book became a bestseller, maybe Dennis could arrange for all of us to attend legitimately.

. . . . .

An hour later, as a young woman served hot coffee, the Ancient Order of Hibernians passed by, bagpipes fore and aft, and I looked around for Dennis and Holly Halligan. She now stood at the north end of the steps, deep in a private and, apparently, serious conversation with a chic woman in her late fifties, swathed in head-to-toe mink. I hoped that none of our fellow guests were animal-rights activists who'd squirreled away a bottle of ink or a pocketful of paint to throw all over the likes of Holly and her new friend.

Dennis was nowhere in sight.

"Those are my people." Modesty pointed to the Hibernians. She'd remained unusually quiet so far, intensely scrutinizing the parade.

"I didn't know you were of Irish descent," I said.

"Neither did I until recently. While I was out in Utah

researching for my current assignment, I went to Salt Lake City to check my roots. The Mormons have super technology. And their computer files are awesome."

"So, what did you discover?" I knew that both of Modesty's parents were dead and her only living relative was her aunt Charity—her mother's sister—who lived in upper Michigan.

"I always thought that Meade was an English name. But turns out, one of Dad's ancestors had been a Druid high priestess. She lived in the south of ancient Hibernia. Near where County Mayo is today."

"Wow! And on your mother's side?"

"Well, Aunt Charity has told me that family history. Mom's people came from Transylvania. In the mountains. The real Count Dracula had the same bloodline."

Why was I not surprised? No wonder Modesty liked to dress in shroudlike garments. And stay up all night. "I guess that explains your gift for gothic horror novels."

"Yeah. And it's the main reason I became a vegetarian. Why take chances, you know?" Modesty sighed. "And I avoid shows like *ER*; the sight of all that blood excites me. Makes me thirsty."

All of the members of Ghostwriters Anonymous have agreed that Modesty has no sense of humor. God knows she never tells—and seldom laughs at—a joke, but maybe she has been putting us on all these years. Druid on one side. Transylvanian on the other. Sounded like a punch line to me.

I felt an arm slip around my shoulder. "Why don't you and Modesty come and meet Senator Fione's wife," Dennis said as his touch traveled to my toes. Would my feet ever stop reacting to this man?

"Where have you been?" I asked, then wished I hadn't.

"Working the steps, Jake." Dennis grinned. "There are a lot of contacts, here." Then the three of us walked over to where Holly stood next to the attractive, dark-haired woman wearing the fur of many dead minks.

Dennis made the introductions, and Edwina Fione extended a slim hand, encased in a soft, pale beige, doeskin glove. Her small, glossy brown, designer shoulder-strap bag, made from alligator skin, brushed against my arm. I glanced down. Sure enough: matching shoes.

"Delighted to meet you, Ms. O'Hara," Mrs. Fione said in a low, cultured, pricey, prep-school type of voice as Modesty snorted in my left ear. The senator's wife then turned her smile in Modesty direction. I braced myself.

"You're a menace to animals," Modesty began, but another blare of trumpets and a clash of cymbals, introducing Our Lady of Victory's marching band's brassy—and loud—interpretation of "McNamara's Band" had rendered her inaudible to all but me.

· · · · ·

Twenty minutes later Modesty and I were deeply entrenched in the Blessed Virgin Sodality as we marched up Fifth Avenue to the Plaza. Rebuffed by the police as we'd attempted to cross the avenue and slowed to a crawl by the crowds of spectators, media, and sundry party-hearty types as we'd tried to walk north on the sidewalk, we'd decided to join the parade. Dennis and Holly had opted to return to the Rolls. If he ever got to make a right turn on Madison, I figured Dennis would be cruising for a spot nearer to the Plaza for hours. They, too, should have joined the Blessed Virgin Sodality.

"After your vicious kick to shut me up," Modesty said as she disentangled herself from the Sodality's blue-and-white banner that the wind had whipped into her hair, "did you hear what that buyer of murdered minks said to the Charon of cremation?"

We'd passed Tiffany's on the right and were coming up to Bergdorf's on the left. The Plaza was less than a block away.

"No, what?"

"Well, when Edwina Fione was saying good-bye, she told Holly Halligan that she couldn't ever remember looking forward to any cruise—and she'd been on hundreds during her lifetime—as much as she was to the one that Holly had arranged."

"Jeez!" I said. "She'll be dead by the time that ship sets sail. Why would anyone be looking forward to her own funeral?"

Modesty brushed snow from her hair and the last of her shamrocks fell to the ground.

"Maybe she didn't book the total-concept cremation cruise for herself. Maybe old Edwina is the designated flinger . . . and someone else's ashes will be traveling in the urn."

The flags in front of the Plaza flapped as if to welcome us.

Three

The annual Greater New York Crime Writers' Conference was scheduled to run from March 17 through March 19. Mystery writers from all over the state would be gathering at the Plaza Hotel on the one day of the year when Manhattan's traffic was—literally—backed up to Jackson Heights.

I love the Plaza. A symbol of old-world elegance. Of order and serenity. As a kid, when Mom had read to me about the adventures of Kay Thompson's Eloise, I wanted to live there, too. Hang out in a suite and order room service for the rest of my life. Play hearts with the doormen. Dine on tea and cake every afternoon in the Palm Court. And, despite Ivana's redecorating binge, it still sounded like a good move.

But today, the lobby had turned into a zoo. Filled with sundry literary animals. Barking, railing, or roaring at the event's longtime coordinator, Donald Jay, tearing into him for starting the conference on St. Patrick's Day.

Watching the action, Modesty said, "This time our

always incompetent coordinator has totally lost it. If we weren't getting two free nights in a Plaza suite, I'd strike! Plotting Someone Else's Murder, indeed! What a weird wordless panel we'll be. How can this man expect us to cite examples of our successful plotting when he knows we're gagged by stronger-than-the-confessional's-seal confidentiality agreements and can't discuss any of the books we've ever ghosted?"

A woman wearing a coat of primary colors almost assaulted the frail Donald with her handbag. I cringed. "You know, I thought this might be fun as well as free, and I knew Mom and Gypsy Rose were itching to meet Senator Fione. They both just loved his *Death of a Filibuster*. Mom thinks it's great that a sixty-something senator could revamp himself into an author. But this is a mob scene I could have skipped." I looked around for Mom and Gypsy Rose. "And how about Donald Jay's timing? It looks like letting all these murder-mystery writers loose on Fifth Avenue during the St. Patrick's Day Parade could end up a bigger, bloodier mess than the St. Valentine's Day Massacre."

"Who is that woman beating up on Donald?" Modesty asked. "She's double his size." I detected a smidgen of pleasure in her voice.

"That's Carita Magenta," Gypsy Rose said. She and Mom, who were followed by a bellhop pushing a trolley filled with all of our overnight bags, had managed to find us 'midst the madding crowd. Gypsy Rose kissed Modesty and me, and continued. "The self-described Empress of Aura. However, I think of her as the color-me-comatose girl. Talk about scraping the bottom of the pit of parapsychology. Carita's self-help books should be banned as dangerous to the reader's mental health. God help us all, she's going to be on my panel."

My mother carried a picnic basket filled with sandwiches, cookies, fruit, a large thermos, and cups. "The Plaza charges three dollars for a cup of coffee and no one could make it through the Emerald Society to a deli. Come on, we've picked up the key to Gypsy Rose's room, let's go have some lunch."

"Mom, you're the greatest!"

My mother smiled. "Haven't I been telling you that for years?"

We followed the bellhop as he attempted to clear a path to the elevator. Donald Jay was trapped in the center of the three-deep crowd of complainers surrounding the reservation desk.

"Who gave the cat burglar the bridal suite?" Donald's scream was loud enough to be heard in Chicago. He'd directed it at a young, reed-thin brunette whose teased hair contrasted sharply with her otherwise mousy appearance. She stood at his side, her eyes staring down at her feet.

"That unfortunate woman is his new assistant," Modesty said. "They change every year. This one's name is Wanda Sparks. Though *she* certainly doesn't."

Wanda said, "Ask Ashley Butler. She's the one who coordinated the hotel-room assignments." I figured that Wanda had enough spark in her to immediately pass the blame along to the Crime Conference's glamorous public-relations person.

"I deserve no less," Donald growled. "It's my karma for hiring two women with more hair than brains. Dumb and Dumber. That's my team. Now go peel that old has-been Maurice Welch off his stool in the Oak Room. He's on his third double vodka." Dismissing Wanda, Donald Jay then shoved his way through the crowd and walked smack into me, knocking my shoulder bag to the floor.

And just kept on strutting. As I was reaching for the right insult to turn him into toast, Holly Halligan and Dennis Kim joined us.

My mother, fluttering around the former movie star like a teenage fan, asked Holly for her autograph. Gypsy Rose then invited Dennis and Holly to share our small repast and Dennis offered to order champagne and caviar to help stretch the menu. He and Holly were parked all the way over on Second Avenue; they'd worked up quite a thirst getting here.

Finally, we all boarded the elevator. Holly Halligan focused her full attention on Mom and Gypsy Rose. "Have you lovely ladies made your funeral arrangements yet?"

Just before the door shut, I saw Carita Magenta interrupt Wanda Sparks's mission to retrieve Maurice Welch from his bar stool, grabbing her by her thin right arm and pulling her off into a corner. Carita's flushed, full face matched the red blocks in her coat. Wanda's eyes were still downcast.

When Gypsy Rose Liebowitz had agreed to appear on a panel, she decided to close her New Age bookstore for two days and enjoy a mini Manhattan holiday, courtesy of the Crime Conference. First she'd upgraded to a beautiful, huge two-room suite on the top floor. And then had invited Mom to share it with her.

No heavy-handed Trump touches here. The eighteenth-century French furniture was upholstered in soft tones of aquamarine and an off-white, tinged with a hint of the same aquamarine. The highly polished oak floors had strategically placed Persian carpets, and crystal chandeliers dangled from the twelve-foot ceilings. Chair rails, ornate moldings, flocked wallpaper, and sconces featuring gilded cherubs, transported us back to the elegance of the Plaza's past glory. A Louis XIV writing desk and handsome armchair, covered in matching aquamarine satin brocade, faced one floor-to-ceiling window. An off-white satin brocade love seat faced the other. Both windows offered a northeast view. I could see the lake in Central Park as well as the parade passing the reviewing stand that ran from Sixty-first to Sixty-fifth Street, along Fifth Avenue.

Gypsy Rose spread out the food, Dennis popped the champagne, and my mother rated the bathroom. Mom was an expert on New York City ladies' rooms. "Honestly, it's nicer than the Waldorf. I do believe this is the biggest and best john I've ever seen. And have you ever seen so much marble? I give it five stars. You know, there are two rooms. Each with a phone and a television set. I can't wait to take a bath tonight. Did you see those fluffy white terrycloth robes? I think I'll rent one of Holly's old ski movies and watch it from the tub!"

Holly said, "I'll just leave some Ashes Away brochures for you to flip through while you're relaxing in the warm water. I'm telling you, Maura, it's the only way to go!"

My mother made a face and sipped her champagne. "Or maybe I'll rent *Casablanca*." I had a feeling that she was beginning to find Holly as irritating as "Danny Boy."

"What's with Wanda?" I asked. "Poor thing, she seems scared to death."

Modesty frowned and pulled her boots off. "Wanda's a ghostwriter, but she doesn't go to meetings!"

"Oh God!" I said. "Trying to cope with her anonymity all alone. No wonder she looked so pained."

"Well," Dennis said, "she's not working for any of my clients. Not that I'd tell you if she were." I choked on his words. Dennis Kim had his clients take every secrecy pledge known to man or God—except for a blood oath—and I wouldn't put that past him. "Are you okay, Jake?" He handed me a glass of champagne and went back to what he was saying, "But rumor has it that Wanda's the ghost behind a current blockbuster."

"Not my *Murder at MGM,* I wrote every word of that," Holly said, and stood up. "You all will have to excuse me. I'm going to my room to get ready for my panel." She took her glass of champagne with her.

I took a gulp of mine. "That's enough to make a ghost sick! Knowing your book's on the best-seller list—with someone else's name on the cover. Modesty, let's invite her to our next Ghostwriters Anonymous meeting. I think Wanda Sparks needs a support group."

Gypsy Rose passed me a tuna on rye. "Lord love a duck, I hope she's not Carita Magenta's ghost. As dreadful as Carita's books are, Ashley Butler told me over cocktails the other night that she doesn't believe Ms. Color-Me-Comatose writes them herself."

Modesty reached for a vegetarian wrap and said, "Gypsy Rose, why on earth were you out drinking with the world's biggest Barbie doll?"

"I wasn't *out drinking* with her, Modesty," Gypsy Rose said. "Ashley Butler and I met at the Algonquin to discuss publicity for the parapsychology panel. And I lobbied, to no avail, to have that charlatan Carita Magenta removed."

Gypsy Rose is the most open and honorable woman I know, as well as Carnegie Hill's favorite psychic. A leggy redhead, with wild, curly hair, a round, shapely figure, and a flare for fashion, she's a siren at sixty. And a smart businesswoman, who owns and operates a successful bookstore/tearoom on the corner of Ninety-third and Madison, where New Age mavens often lecture. My mother works there part-time. Gypsy Rose and Mom have been best friends for over a quarter of a century, ever since we moved into the roomy old co-op on Ninety-second Street that Mom had inherited from her great-aunt.

Some of Gypsy Rose's more successful séances have made me rethink reincarnation and other odd ghost stories. Via Zelda Fitzgerald, Gypsy Rose's spirit guide, Mom receives messages from and gossip about Jack O'Hara's "lifestyle" in the world beyond. Though Mom had been long divorced from Dad when he passed over to another plane, upon his death, she canonized him. Now we hear he's taking dancing lessons from Fred Astaire. I don't know what to make of all this. But I do know if Gypsy Rose Liebowitz thinks Carita Magenta's a fake, she probably is.

"Jake, finish that last oatmeal cookie," my mother said. "It's almost one o'clock. Let's go down to the Grand Ballroom. I'd like to get a good seat so I can see Charlie Fione up close."

Dennis said, "Oh, I'll be happy to introduce you and Gypsy Rose to him, Maura. The senator has an eye for pretty women."

I stuffed the oatmeal cookie in my mouth.

Four

Over three hundred authors, wannabe writers, agents, editors, book doctors, homicide detectives, Hollywood producers, as well as assorted arson, poison, and firearms experts had descended upon the floor of the Grand Ballroom. No one wanted to miss the opening, celebrity-filled panel: Turn Your Career into Murder. All three hundred were talking at once.

The third panelist, sharing the spotlight with Holly Halligan and Senator Charlie Fione, would be the man that most of the attendees—including me—wanted to chat up. The recently paroled cat burglar, Rickie Romero. A charming thief, Rickie had caught the public's fancy when, during his trial ten years ago, America learned he'd endowed a shelter on Eleventh Avenue for Hell's Kitchen's homeless. His strong resemblance to Fabio hadn't hurt his popularity either.

Romero's book, *Cat on Trump Tower's Roof*, starred a gentleman thief whose assorted victims—wealthy widows, dilettante debutantes, and tyro trophy wives—all had fallen in love with him. When Rickie's antihero was arrested for murdering an heiress in bed, all the formerly bejeweled women whom he'd romanced, then robbed, rushed to his defense. Many critics considered it, like so many first novels, to be autobiographical and declared it to be a fun read. My mother agreed and, since I hadn't read it yet, had given me her rave review. Romero's mystery was outselling Halligan's *Murder at MGM* and Fione's *Death of a Filibuster*.

Holly, now dressed in a chic black pantsuit, with her silver hair piled high on her head, every inch the movie star, greeted us as soon as we crossed the threshold. "I've saved five seats in the front row; follow me." She glided toward the front of the huge room, bowing and waving to the crowd. We, her entourage, trailed behind.

A staggering Maurice Welch, the dean emeritus of international suspense, leaning on the slim shoulder of Wanda Sparks, preceded us down the aisle. Pasty-faced and hunched, he looked sick. I guessed that Wanda had been baby-sitting the literary *enfant terrible* for the last hour or so, keeping him dry.

As Wanda and Maurice arrived at the front row, Rickie Romero, dashing in designer black wool, his smart blazer adorned with a green carnation, jumped up from his aisle seat and insisted that Welch take it. The rumpled Maurice collapsed as if the air had gone out of his balloon. Then Romero swept a flushed Sparks off to the sidelines. Dennis sat next to Maurice, and Modesty, Mom, Gypsy Rose, and I filled the next four chairs.

Fascinated, I stretched my neck to watch Wanda Sparks and Rickie Romero. They now stood, heads together, talking, near a buffet table set up against the west wall. Suddenly Wanda jerked away from Romero and ran off toward the French doors.

Holly took her place at the head table to loud cheers.
An even louder roar from the crowd greeted the arrival
of the senior senator from New York. Tall, portly but
well tailored, his thick gray hair slightly awry, he strode
down the aisle to loud cheers and a few scattered boos.
Not everyone here had voted for Charlie Fione. Me, for
one. Though I'd never told my mother. Edwina walked
at his side. Both were smiling and waving, working the
room like they would a political rally. The senator sat
to Holly's left at the speaker's table; his wife perched,
as if ready to flee, directly across the aisle from Maurice
Welch.

Modesty, no doubt at my mother's request, climbed
over Dennis and Maurice Welch and darted up to the
head table, Mom's camcorder in hand, to videotape the
senator and the former movie star just as Rickie Romero,
clutching a coffee cup from the buffet table, joined his
two co-panelists. Rickie kissed Holly's hand, then sat to
her right. The audience, acknowledging the three best-
selling authors manning the Turn Your Career into Murder panel, went wild. And Modesty grabbed the photo
op.

The Crime Writers' president, Hunter Green, took the
podium, signaling the official start of the thirty-fifth annual Greater New York Crime Writers' Conference. Receiving a rousing welcome, he held the group's total
attention and respect.

Hunter's a honey. I've long considered his books to
be the finest examples of true-crime writing since *In
Cold Blood*. This afternoon, in keeping with both his
name and St. Patrick's Day, the African-American Hunter was all in green—from his kelly bowler to his olive
corduroy jeans. On lanky, handsome Hunter, the out-
landish garb looked great.

When Hunter announced that the warlock who'd been scheduled for Gypsy Rose's out-of-this-world panel was stuck in Salem, and added that Hunter himself—having just finished covering a vampire murder trial—would fill in, Gypsy Rose clapped the loudest. Then stage-whispered, "What a coup, Jake! I'm sharing a panel with an Edgar winner!"

"Maybe that will make Carita Magenta somewhat easier to swallow," I said.

Gypsy Rose giggled. "About as easy as a dose of castor oil. Thank god, the warlock's car broke down. One nut per panel is all I can stomach."

At that moment Venus DeMill, the glamorous, aging author of a murder-mystery series set in ancient Rome, dressed in Versace, and quarreling none too quietly with Carita Magenta, arrived late and, disturbing the people already seated there, claimed two chairs in the second row. Carita squeezed her considerable bulk into a seat directly behind me. Having removed her coat of many colors, she now wore green tights and an oversized sweatshirt with KISS ME I'M IRISH! emblazoned across her breasts. When Carita had managed to contain her girth, she reached across my back and grabbed the collar of Gypsy Rose's coral cashmere dress. As Gypsy Rose, obviously startled, swung around, Carita yelled, "Tell your friends to hold their water, there's a leprechaun in the ladies' room."

Hunter Green handed the mike over to Donald Jay, who spent the next ten minutes reviewing the conference rules, managing to transform the Plaza's ballroom into a cross between a college dorm and an SS camp. Eliciting grunts and groans from the attendees, he concluded with, "If you have any complaints, see Wanda Sparks or Ashley Butler; that is, if you can ever find either of them."

Maurice Welch, apparently resurrected, poked my mother in the arm and announced with a booming Brooklyn accent, "That half-baked potato's stuffed with crap, ain't he, Blondie?"

To my delight, Mom replied, "You got that right!"

Donald Jay finally shut up. And his restless audience did, too. Now all eyes were locked on the head table. The senior senator from New York, the ex-movie-star-turned-television-pitch-person, and the retired cat burglar smiled back at their fans.

Yet another haunting rendition of "Danny Boy," this time performed by what sounded like a score of bagpipers parading along Fifth Avenue, echoed through the ballroom. My mother said, "For God's sake, can't they let that Irishman rest in peace?"

Seemingly from out of nowhere, a lively leprechaun appeared and placed a pitcher of green beer in front of Charlie Fione. The senator laughed, leaned into his mike, and, affecting an Irish brogue, said, "Happy St. Patrick's Day. And may we all be in heaven a half hour before the devil knows we're dead!" Fione graciously filled Halligan and Romero's glasses before his own.

Holly clicked her glass against Charlie's and Rickie's, then held it up as if to toast the audience, saying, "Erin Go Bragh!" Shouts of approval swept through the ballroom as the panelists raised their beers to their lips.

Charlie Fione screamed first. Then rolled from his seat, grabbing at his throat, and landed, clutching his stomach, on the Persian carpet. Holly Halligan's mouth formed a perfect O, but nothing came out. On my feet, stepping on Gypsy Rose's pumps, trying to get to the head table, I watched Holly tumble to the floor, thrashing and flaying. Not a pretty picture. Rickie Romero shook as if in violent denial, then crashed face first into the bowl of shamrocks on the table in front of him. Modesty, who'd scampered out of the row before me, videotaped the ghastly scene while Dennis dialed 911 and my mother cried, "God help us! Someone has killed them all!"

Five

As the medical examiner for the City of New York—he'd been scheduled for a Cause of Death seminar at five—checked for pulses, Dennis Kim, Hunter Green, and a suddenly, surprisingly, sober Maurice Welch kept pandemonium at bay, instructing the Plaza staff to see that no one touched the bodies or left the room. However, Gypsy Rose said, "I saw that leprechaun disappear through the French doors right after delivering the pitcher of beer."

Edwina Fione knelt, silently, at her husband's side, head bowed as if in prayer. Carita Magenta had fainted and was now stuck in her chair as Venus DeMill frantically attempted to revive her. Several of the crime reporters from the local newspapers were on their cell phones. Others were writing their leads.

Donald Jay, his pasty face now flushed a bright red, paced back and forth in front of the podium. "Where the hell is Ashley Butler?" He directed his question to Hunter Green, but, clearly neither expecting or wanting an answer, continued in a voice a decibel lower than hysteria. "We have to issue some sort of a statement. A press release. That's her job. Those media vultures will be all over this! I need Ashley to explain to America's mystery fans how three famous authors could end up murdered at my Crime Writers' Conference!" Though I choked back a giggle, Donald had spoken without irony.

My mother fished a bottle of springwater out of her tote bag and passed it to Venus DeMill, who then dampened her Hermès scarf and placed it on Carita's forehead. Just how much money did Venus make on those ancient-history mysteries? Why hadn't she interrupted her ministrations long enough to walk over to the sideboard and pick up a napkin to use as Magenta's headache rag?

I watched the ME gently close Senator Fione's eyes, then bend over Holly Halligan's contorted face. "They've been poisoned," I said to Modesty. I felt like I might throw up. "They're all dead!"

The coroner confirmed my first call. "A slight smell of bitter almonds. Looks like cyanide—lots of it to act so fast." He moved on to Rickie's inert form. But, boy, was I wrong on my second. Holly Halligan and Charlie Fione, indeed, had died in several, ugly, painful minutes, but Rickie Romero had been playing possum.

When the ME touched the pulse in Romero's neck, the cat burglar raised his handsome face from the bowl of shamrocks and smiled. The coroner jumped away, almost losing his balance. The audience emitted a collective shriek. Carita Magenta, who'd just come to, passed out again.

"What the hell is going on?" Dennis shouted.

"Just why did you play dead?" Maurice Welch asked,

pulling a pad and pen from his wrinkled jacket's pocket. "What was your motivation?"

Rickie laughed. "You think I'd give a crazed mass murderer a second chance? That creep might have had a gun. I probably saved my butt by pretending I'd been poisoned. And put your notes away, Mr. Welch. I'm writing this book myself."

A booming voice came from the back of the ballroom. "Are you a clairvoyant as well as a cat burglar?" Detective Lieutenant Ben Rubin, chief of homicide at Manhattan's Nineteenth Precinct and the current man in my life, strode down the aisle and introduced himself to Rickie Romero. "As I understand it, a room full of witnesses saw you raise the glass to your mouth. Did you suspect a cyanide cocktail? Or do you have an allergy to green beer?"

Rickie shrugged. "Well, I guess you could call it an allergy. I'm a recovering alcoholic, Detective. No way would I have swallowed that beer. Sometimes it's easier to pretend that you've taken a sip than it is to explain why you're not drinking. Especially on St. Patrick's Day."

"You're just a great pretender, aren't you, Romero?" I could hear Ben's controlled rage.

"Exactly, Detective, exactly!" Rickie Romero, seemingly in total agreement with Ben Rubin's assessment, flashed his perfect teeth.

Ten minutes later Donald Jay stepped up the podium to announce, officially, that the conference had been canceled, but Ben warned everyone in the room not to plan on leaving the city. The police would be speaking to all three hundred attendees over the next few days. Those of us who lived in the city could check out of our rooms, after giving our home addresses to the policemen at the door. But a visibly agitated Donald Jay would have to honor the out-of-town writers' reservations at the Plaza even though his show never got off the ground. And, as Maurice Welch said to my mother, with what could pass for glee, "Dear old Donald may lose his job."

As the bodies were about to be tagged and bagged, Ben ordered the stragglers out of the ballroom. Dennis invited Mom, Gypsy Rose, Modesty, and me to join him for tea in the Palm Court. My mother, looking wan, accepted for all of us. Feeling both surprised and guilty, I realized that I was starving.

The soft lights, beautiful furnishings, and old-world charm of the open Palm Court, set in the center of the Plaza lobby, soothed my jangled nerves. Still I couldn't erase the images of Holly Halligan's last gasp or Charlie Fione holding his stomach. What a rotten way to go. Ben seemed to have targeted Rickie Romero as the killer, holding him as a material witness, but I wasn't so sure. Call it a hunch. I wondered what my tea companions were thinking. With this bunch, I wouldn't have to pry out suspicions, but we did wait until the scones had been served.

"Do you believe the murderer is a crazy celebrity stalker?" My mother began the recap. "Or do you think Rickie did it?"

Gypsy Rose had closed her eyes. Probably chatting about clues with Zelda Fitzgerald. Opening those Sophia Loren eyes, my favorite fortune-teller said, "I've received a strong impression that neither of those explanations is correct."

"Me, too," I said. "And I'm not even psychic! When could Rickie have spiked the beer with cyanide?"

Modesty examined the tea tray. "I heard the senator say something strange to Holly Halligan. And I have it on tape." She popped a scone in her mouth.

"What?" Mom, Gypsy Rose, Dennis, and I asked in unison.

"Senator Fione said, 'A hell of a place for a reunion, isn't it, Helen Mary Houlihan?' And he didn't look happy. For that matter, neither did she."

"So they knew each other!" I said.

"Yep." Modesty spread strawberry jam on another scone. "Furthermore, I think both Hunter Green and Donald Jay overheard what the senator said to Holly."

"You have to turn that tape over to the police," Dennis said.

"Done," Modesty muttered through a full mouth.

"What about the leprechaun?" my mother asked. "Was he an accomplice? Or the killer?"

Gypsy Rose nodded. "And what had he been doing in the ladies' room? Remember what Carita Magenta said."

Pouring more tea, Dennis said, "Hunter Green had a confrontation with Rickie Romero in the men's room shortly before the panel got started. Something about having faith."

"Lots of action going down in the rest rooms," Gypsy Rose said. "But then everyone at the conference wanted a chance to stroke that cat burglar."

"Did anyone notice Rickie Romero with Wanda Sparks?" I asked.

"I did, Jake." Gypsy Rose frowned. " 'Fizzles' might be a better name for Ms. Sparks, but no question, Rickie did seem interested in her."

Dennis said, "Another thing, Holly mentioned to me that Maurice Welch has booked an Ashes Away party boat for his last fling."

"I think Holly Halligan was a ghoul," Modesty said.

"Now that's she's dead, she's in her element."

"Okay. So what do a former movie star, a powerful United States senator, and a cat burglar have in common?" I asked. "Are we looking for one killer with three motives? And if so, are those motives somehow tied together? Or are we looking for a killer with just one motive—but one strong enough to have him murder two other innocent people just for his convenience or, maybe, our confusion?"

"Or could we be looking for more than one killer?" Dennis asked.

I felt an overwhelming urge. "Well, if each of us did just the least bit of digging, we might . . ."

My mother glared at me. "Don't even think about it, Jake! Let Ben Rubin and his homicide department solve these murders. Promise me! Now!"

Gypsy Rose came through with the save. "Perhaps, just a small séance . . ."

Six

The St. Patrick's Day parade veered right at Eighty-sixth Street. The snow had stopped. And, along Third Avenue, many of the units had dispersed into the local watering holes. Dennis Kim weaved the Rolls around the masses who'd migrated up to Ninety-second Street and deposited Mom and me in front of our co-op.

A town house, built in the early twentieth century, the building had been converted into apartments just before WW II. But its original white stone facade, featuring rounded architectural lines and bay windows, remained intact. On this damp, chilly late afternoon, even a Plaza suite would have been a poor second choice to the comfort of our house on Ninety-second.

Emotionally and physically exhausted, I smiled as we rode the tiny mahogany-and-brass elevator up to the second floor. "You know, Mom, Toto had it right. There really is no place like home!"

Carnegie Hill had become a neighborhood in the early 1900s, when Andrew Carnegie built his mansion on the corner of Fifth Avenue and Ninety-first, turning what high society had scorned as "too far uptown" and "no-man's-land" into a chic residential area. His mansion now housed the Cooper-Hewitt Museum—a branch of the Smithsonian—and its garden was one of my favorite hangouts.

All of the Hill enchanted me. From Central Park on the west to the bustle of Lexington Avenue on the east. From the movie houses and ethnic restaurants on Eighty-sixth Street, the southern border, to the great mix of Art Deco, Romanesque, and Beaux Arts buildings gracing the blocks leading up to Ninety-sixth, its northern border.

The neighborhood, an architectural jewel, included some of the priciest real estate in Manhattan. Actors, directors, brokers, politicians, talk-show hosts, and a former president's daughter resided in its multimillion-dollar town houses and apartments. Many of Carnegie Hill's residents were so wealthy they'd stopped counting; a few, like Mom and me, owned their co-ops outright but were struggling to keep up with the maintenance and taxes.

Money, or the lack thereof, had kept me a ghostwriter. And money management was a skill I'd never mastered. Plotting other authors' mysteries left me with little time and less energy to create my own. My last two assignments—though well paid—had been murder. Maybe being a ghost means living dangerously. As Modesty had observed this morning: Death doesn't take a holiday. I sank into an armchair and closed my eyes. The faces of today's dead came back to haunt me.

"I'd really like to talk to you, Jake." My mother was circling the couch. I hoped to God that she wasn't about to launch into another analysis of my single state and/

or the status of my relationship with Ben Rubin. The truth was I didn't know where our romance, if that was what it was, might be going. I suspected that Dennis Kim's gold-flecked eyes and annoyingly magic touch, as well as my fear of commitment, had contributed to the confusion. Still Ben and I did have a special something—nameless but intense—that we'd shared for the last nine months. We'd met during one murder case and quarreled over another. Currently, we were cautiously "courting"—to use my mother's archaic term. Meanwhile Mom, somewhat to my chagrin, seemed to be much further along in her relationship with the retired district attorney for the City of New York, Aaron Rubin, a widower and Ben's father.

But Ben and I weren't the ones on my mother's mind.

"Even though they weren't young, I'll bet that Holly Halligan and Senator Fione thought they had a lot of time ahead of them. I've been thinking that I did, too. But look what happened: two people poisoned in the prime of their life!"

Only my mother, seemingly foxy forever, could say, in all sincerity, that a seventy-four-or-maybe-more-year-old woman and a senator in his late sixties were in their prime. I settled in for one of Mom's philosophical monologues, requiring, on my part, only an alert expression and an occasional sage nod.

"Death gives one pause," my mother said, then looked pained when I laughed, providing more than her required response. "Not the deceased, of course, he or she goes on stop—not pause—for eternity. But a survivor tends to halt, reflect, and ask—"

"What's it all about, Alfie?"

"Jake, you're making this very difficult for me."

"Sorry, go ahead, Mom."

"Well, Aaron has—that is—well, life's short, isn't it, darling?"

I nodded, looking, I hoped, alert.

My mother sighed. "Yes, it is. Too damn short. That's why I've decided to accept Aaron's proposal."

Holy God! My mother was about to marry my boyfriend's father! What would this wedding do to my happy home life? Shoving that selfish thought to some dark recess of my soul, I smiled, kissed my mother, and asked, "Do I get to give the bride away?"

Less than three hours later Gypsy Rose had arranged an impromptu engagement dinner. Her ten guests were asked to assemble on Fifth Avenue and Ninety-first Street, then we'd split into two groups to traverse Central Park in horse-drawn carriages and arrive at the Tavern on the Green in time for dinner at eight. Our hostess had style. Straight from her soul. According to my mother, Gypsy Rose had acquired all that panache over several interesting incarnations. Including her most recent past life, during which she had been engaged in a love affair with Edgar Cayce.

The bride and bridegroom elect, together with Mr. Kim, Gypsy Rose, and her ardent admirer, Christian Holmes, the gruff, aging atheist who'd long served as religion editor for *Manhattan Magazine*, rode in the first hansom cab. Ben had called to say he was running late and would meet us at the restaurant, so I shared the second cab with Modesty, Dennis, and Dennis's date for the evening—none other than the literary world's biggest Barbie doll, Ashley Butler. I'd had enough surprises today to last me a lifetime.

"Isn't it romantic?" Ashley was saying in a most irritating drawl. "I thought Dennis and I were going to have a dreary little old business dinner, and suddenly here I am, celebrating a betrothal and riding in a carriage to one of my favorite restaurants."

"What business do you have with Dennis?" Modesty asked. I wanted to kiss her bold face.

Ashley patted her Sears-Tower-high hair. "Why, I'm an author. That is, I will be when my book comes out next summer. Dennis is my attorney." She giggled. "Well, among other things."

Dennis looked like he cheerfully could have strangled her. "Ashley, I never discuss a client's business and my clients never discuss mine." He spoke softly, but tension tightened his jaw. "A confidentiality agreement is an important part of the contract you were scheduled to sign this evening."

"That's my PR persona bursting forth, unbridled." Ashley giggled again. "I'll just switch to my author's hat and shut my mouth!"

"Where was your PR persona hiding this afternoon?" Modesty asked. "Donald Jay seemed lost without it." Maybe I'd marry Modesty.

Ashley must have missed Dennis's frown. "Why, I was in the ladies' room. My, it's pretty! I'd like to have a dress made in the same pattern as the wallpaper. I got to stare at it for a long time." She giggled for a third time. "The tuna fish or the mayonnaise at lunch must have been tainted. It's a bit embarrassing to talk about this in front of a gentleman, but, dear Lord, I was locked in a stall for what seemed like hours."

"Did you happen to see a leprechaun?" I asked.

"That nice Detective Rubin asked me the very same question." Ashley reached across the carriage and gripped my arm. "I did. That is—I saw his black leather boots and his green tights from his knees down. My view, from under the stall's door, was somewhat limited.

Frankly, I'd been feeling so poorly that, at the time, I thought I was hallucinating."

"And what time would that be?" I asked as we pulled up in front of the restaurant's glittering courtyard.

"Oh, Jake, I don't recall. My best guess would be about the same time that the conference was getting started. I do know it was right after Carita Magenta and Venus DeMill had their screaming match over Maurice Welch."

Modesty said, "Well, let's hope you're feeling well enough to enjoy your dinner tonight. You seem to have made an amazing recovery. A stomach upset from food poisoning can last for days. Hey, you didn't drink any of that green beer, did you?"

Ashley totally ignored Modesty's comments, then turning away, extended her hand to Dennis as he reached up to help her out of the carriage.

Even on such a bleak March evening, the main dining room in Tavern on the Green sparkled like sunshine. Though many of my more jaded New York friends have dismissed the place as a tourist trap, I've always gotten a kick out of its glitz and glow. Tonight, however, Ashley's ongoing rave review dramatically diminished the restaurant's charm.

Gypsy Rose, a truly amazing woman, had Dom Pérignon on ice and lobster-salad appetizers on order by the time we arrived. My mother's glow matched the candlelight's. Aaron Rubin, who reminded me of the older gray-haired guy in the Polo ads, couldn't take his eyes off her. Mr. Kim and Christian Holmes were engaged in their ongoing God-versus-Darwin debate. The topic tonight seemed to be predestination.

"Do you believe that Holly Halligan and Charlie Fione actually had a March seventeenth date with Death?"

Christian asked. "An appointment at the Plaza to check out of this world?"

Both Mr. Kim and Gypsy Rose said, "Yes!"

Christian raised a bushy eyebrow, but said nothing.

I decided to switch the conversation from predestination to premeditation. "Did you know the Fiones?" I asked Christian.

"Edwina had been the subject of one of my first *Manhattan* profiles. You know, those in-depth pieces focusing on spirituality in sin city." Christian paused for a sip of champagne. "I met the senator twice. Briefly. Once at a fund-raiser for the main library. Once at their apartment on Park Avenue while I was interviewing his wife."

"Do you think they had a good marriage?" Modesty asked.

"A strange coupling," Christian said. "Edwina, like so many converts, was hyped on heaven. Once she'd embraced Catholicism, she became holier than the Church's hierarchy. Her husband was a cafeteria Catholic. Took what he liked, left the rest on the sideboard."

My mother, probably better informed about Fione family history than Christian Holmes, jumped in. "And they came from two different worlds."

"That's right, Maura." Christian wasn't ready to turn the reins over to Mom. "The senator was a product of Hell's Kitchen. A tough street kid, raised by his mother, he scratched his way through school and won a scholarship to NYU. Edwina was a Carrington of Connecticut, raised in genteel Episcopalian decadence in Westport and educated at Smith. But I believe the marriage was as good as could be expected, considering that Edwina had to swim in Charlie Fione's fishbowl. That man loved living in Macy's window."

"You're mixing your metaphors, there, Christian," Modesty said.

"Well," Gypsy Rose said, "it seems their marriage was good enough for Edwina to call me—at Hunter Green's suggestion—so completely consumed with grief that she felt an overwhelming need to talk to her 'charming Charlie' one last time. She'd expected to be at his bedside to say her good-byes; now she wants me to channel Charlie. On the East River, yet. Edwina's arranged an Ashes Away burial service aboard a chartered boat that will circle Manhattan Island. And honoring her late husband's wishes, she plans on inviting some of his fellow crime writers to the send-off. Of course, she has to wait for his body to be released after the autopsy."

Modesty said, "How about that? Old Edwina will be on deck—aboard that cruise she told Holly Halligan she was so looking forward to—while her 'charming Charlie' will be sailing to his final destination, packed in an urn!"

Seven

I'd spent a miserable night, alternating between long hours of clock-watching wakefulness and a recurring dream starring a leprechaun who raised the skull and crossbones on the good ship *Lollipop* and then forced me to walk the plank. Into an ocean of pink bubble gum. Making swimming impossible. I was drowning in the third replay, when the phone's loud ring saved me from yet another sticky demise. As I picked up the receiver, I remembered that dealing with death always gave me nightmares.

"Sorry I stood you up last night," Ben said.

"Yeah. Well, the maître d' gave us your message. We missed you. And you missed a great dinner."

"Hell, I dined on cold pizza at the morgue."

"I trust not in a room with a view. Are the autopsies finished?"

"Only Senator Fione's. Holly Halligan's on the table as we speak."

I shuddered, thinking of pretty Holly, who, only yesterday, had been so full of septuagenarian sass, song, and salesmanship.

"Cyanide?"

"The cause of death? Yes . . ."

"What, Ben? There's something else, isn't there?"

"Cancer. Charlie Fione had pancreatic cancer. The ME says the senator had less than a month to live."

"Jesus! No wonder Edwina had thought she'd be at his bedside to say good-bye. The widow says she needs to talk to Charlie one last time. She asked Gypsy Rose to conduct a channeling aboard Fione's Ashes Away cruise."

"Is that right? Tell Gypsy Rose I'll be on board."

"When will I be seeing you?"

"Dying to talk about the case, aren't you?" Ben laughed. The man knew me too well. "Okay, let's shoot for dinner tonight. We'll talk this afternoon. And Jake, just think, when my father marries your mother, I'll be your stepbrother. See ya later, sis." He hung up.

. . . . .

My mother was burning English muffins when I walked into the kitchen. "Start with cereal, Jake. Cut up one of those peaches. Mr. Kim said they came from Bolivia." Mom reached for a fork and attacked another muffin.

"So where did you guys go dancing?" I asked, resenting our role reversal that seemed to have started with Mom's engagement announcement.

"Gypsy Rose recommended some new swing dance club down in NoHo. Would you believe that Christian Holmes does a great Lindy Hop? Of course, he came of age long before rock and roll. His generation grew up dancing together, instead of twisting in opposite directions. Unfortunately, he hurt his back throwing Gypsy Rose up in the air during the 'Boogie Woogie Bugle Boy of Company B.' The evening ended early."

By nine o'clock, the bright sunshine had brought the temperature up to sixty degrees. During my power walk in Central Park, I came to three decisions. If Ben balked at taking dancing lessons, I'd drag one of the ghosts along with me. While most of Manhattan had been moving to the retro music of Tommy Dorsey, I'd remained a wallflower. This afternoon, I'd register for classes, then go shopping for saddle shoes. My karate lessons had gotten me into pretty good shape, but I wanted more. I wanted to swing.

My second decision sprang from my gut and was based on my reaction to the poisoning of the panelists. While I love a mystery—and thrive on solving one—I felt I had no option here. Holly Halligan continued to haunt me. Who had wanted her, Charlie Fione, and Rickie Romero dead? Or who wanted one of the three dead and was willing to sacrifice the other two? Ben believed Romero himself had masterminded the plot. Modesty seemed to be leaning toward Edwina, with Ashley Butler running a close second. But neither Ben nor Modesty had any motive in mind. And while I didn't have a clue, I knew I had to find out who the killer was.

The third decision mixed murder with eggs Benedict. I'd have brunch with my three favorite ghosts after this morning's Ghostwriters Anonymous meeting, and then enlist their help in investigating this mystery. I smiled, realizing that Modesty was already hooked.

. . . . .

The Upper East Side chapter of Ghostwriters Anonymous had been meeting at the Jan Hus Church on

Seventy-first Street, just west of First Avenue, on Saturday mornings for almost three years. A bunch of us ghosts had banded together to work a twelve-step program and to learn how to cope with our anonymity. Most of our members were well on their way toward recovering their self-esteem, though some ghosts were sicker than others. But we all shared our suggestions for living a day at a time as unknown and unrecognized writers in New York City's highly visible literary community. And through the years, we'd developed a bond as close as family.

I climbed the stairs to the large, second-floor meeting room, listening to Jane D, a successful how-to-ghost, specializing in spirituality and Juno/Jupiter relationships, complain about her current employer. All of us ghostwriters spent too much time doing that, trying to seize back control of our computer input and forgetting to work the third step, turning our will over to God . . . as we understand Him.

"Honest to heaven, Jake," Jane said. "This time, I'm dealing with a woman spawned in the bowels of hell." Jane was slender, about an inch taller than my five-foot-four, and had big doe eyes. She'd recently had her dark brown hair cut into a pixie, and with her huge black sunglasses perched atop her small, heart-shaped face, she reminded me a bit of Audrey Hepburn in *Roman Holiday*.

I've always preferred the fellowship of the Ghostwriters Anonymous program to working its twelve steps, so I could identify with Jane's feelings. Since I had no suggestions, and no desire to share what I considered to be my woefully inadequate experience, strength, and hope with her, I told Jane that today she looked like Audrey Hepburn. That certainly seemed to cheer her up. And change the conversation, too.

We took our seats in the circle of about twenty fellow ghosts just as they all joined hands for the Serenity Prayer. Too Tall Tom, a handyman ghost and my best friend, was leading the meeting. When he asked if we had any newcomers, anyone who might be attending Ghostwriters Anonymous for the first time, a small voice, belonging to a face that was hidden behind a Big Book, said with great hesitation, "I've never been to a meeting before."

"Would you like to introduce yourself to the group?" Too Tall Tom asked.

Putting the Big Book in her lap, our prospective member said, "I'm Wanda Sparks . . . that is . . . Wanda S. And . . . I'm a ghost who's addicted to anonymity!"

Modesty, sitting next to Wanda, flashed me a thumbs-up. It couldn't be coincidence that this morning the group's focus was on step twelve: having had a spiritual awakening as a result of these steps, we tried to carry this message to other ghosts, and to practice these principles in all of our affairs. Following tradition, Modesty M had made a twelfth-step call, in order to bring our program's message to a fellow ghostwriter who was still suffering from anonymity all alone. And then dragged her to a meeting. It also was no coincidence that Modesty knew just how much I wanted to question Wanda Sparks about the cyanide poisonings.

Most new members are shy about sharing. I don't think I said a word about my feelings until I'd celebrated three months. After the first ninety days recovering ghosts are given Casper balloons to remind us that anonymity can be fun. On that day I'd opened up.

Wanda S had no such reservations about dumping all her garbage at her first meeting. When Too Tall Tom

invited her to share, she tossed her trash right into the
center of the circle.

"The thing is, I'm a lowly administrative assistant,"
Wanda began, her eyes downcast. Several ghosts nodded
encouragingly. We'd all had our problems with self-
worth. "But I've always had this flair for writing. I've
edited the Greater New York Crime Writers' newsletter
for the last six months, but Donald Jay takes the credit.
Of course, my dream was to publish a book. Like a
murder, you know? Anyhow, one day I mentioned this
to Hunter Green. He's an okay guy and he'd seen me
struggling while Jay grabbed the byline. Hunter hooked
me up with this real famous crook who'd been spending
his time in prison, trying to write a mystery."

I started, spilling some of my coffee on Jane's shoe.
She shrugged, as if it was of no consequence, but then
carefully wiped off her leather slingback pump with a
moist towelette that she readily located in her purse.
God, if possible, Jane was even more anal-retentive than
my mother. I turned my attention back to Wanda.

"The story sizzled; the thief did, too," Wanda said.
"So I became a ghost. Signed a confidentiality
agreement. Wrote the goddamn book and now it's a
goddamn best-seller. My employer got out of jail; he's
a goddamn celebrity too busy to bother with his former
ghost. And nobody knows my name!" She burst into
tears. The ghosts gathered round, showering her with
affirmations of love and support.

. . . . .

Wanda couldn't join us for brunch; she was
running late. Donald Jay had insisted that she be at his
side while he haggled with the Plaza's management over
refunds. But before she'd taken off, Modesty had agreed

to act as Wanda's sponsor. Sort of a Ghostwriter Anonymous big sister, who served as a mentor, leading a newcomer through the steps. I chose not to question Modesty's motives. If Wanda's relationship with Romero was connected to these poisonings, I knew Modesty would ferret out that information before they got to step two.

Too Tall Tom, Jane, Modesty, and I sat at a window table in Sarabeth's Kitchen on the corner of Ninety-second and Madison, diagonally across the street from my house. We would have gone to Gypsy Rose's bookstore/tearoom, but Modesty had insisted on having a Sarabeth muffin. They were the best—and possibly the most expensive—muffins in Manhattan.

"That was cool, getting Wanda to come to a meeting, Modesty," I said.

"You two didn't use our recovery program to further your own ends, did you?" Jane sounded aghast.

"How could you suggest such a thing?" Too Tall Tom said, winking at me. "Get your mind out of the gutter, Jane."

Flustered, Jane retreated for a moment into the menu, then said, "I'll have the French toast and a double hot chocolate. But I know that by dessert, Jake will have us all playing detective again. Not that I mind. Delving into murder excites my spirit; I just don't want to compromise my ethics. Or those of another ghost."

"Okay," I said. "No breaking and entering for Jane."

Too Tall Tom, who had a lot of space to fill, ordered two meals: Belgian waffles and corn-beef hash. Modesty opted for a vegetable salad and a banana-nut muffin and I, as I had decided earlier, went with the eggs Benedict.

"So, have you heard from Ben?" Too Tall Tom asked.

"I'm fascinated by this case. What does Detective Hunk say?"

I filled the three of them in on the results of the senator's autopsy; then Modesty updated Jane and Too Tall Tom on the conference killings . . . and who'd said or done anything that might be deemed as suspicious. By time she'd finished, our food arrived.

Digging into his hash, Too Tall Tom said, "I read in this morning's *Daily News* that Rickie Romero was released after questioning. Does Ben think he's the killer?"

"Yes, I think he does." I added pepper to my eggs. "But I don't."

"Might that be because Rickie's such a heartthrob?" Too Tall Tom asked. "That man is simply too divine and, of course, his being a cat burglar just makes him so like a young Cary Grant, doesn't it?"

Modesty stabbed a cucumber. "Forget about Romero's looks! We've got some serious contenders in this killing field. Take Ashley Butler. Did she see the leprechaun in the bathroom or was *she* the leprechaun? Same goes for Wanda Sparks. She, too, claims to have seen a little green man in the john, but interestingly enough, neither Wanda or Ashley can alibi the other."

"Maybe," I said, "Ashley had been locked in the stall the entire time that Wanda was in there."

"Incidentally, Jake," Modesty said, "last night, Dennis Kim dropped that human harvest-of-hair Ashley Butler off before driving me home."

I felt the color flood my face. "What makes you think I'd be the least bit interested in that piece of information?"

Jane and Too Tall Tom's laughter lingered long enough to give me my answer.

Over café au laits and sticky buns, we planned our strategy. Too Tall Tom took Maurice Welch. "I understand he's still in the cupboard, darling."

"No way!" I said. "He's engaged to Venus DeMill."

Too Tall Tom laid one of his killer smiles on me. "A lavender couple."

"A what?" Jane asked.

"Like Janet Gaynor and Adrian," Too Tall Tom said. When Jane still looked blank, he continued, "A famous Hollywood couple in the thirties. She won the first ever Best Actress Oscar. For *Seventh Heaven*—1927, I think. He was a famous MGM fashion designer. Their marriage was a cover story."

It was my turn to look blank. "Are you inferring that Maurice Welch and Venus DeMill are both gay?"

"I imply, darling, you infer." Too Tall Tom laughed. "Or is that the other way around? Anyway, if you really want to know about Venus DeMill's sexual preference, ask Carita Magenta."

Jane said she'd track down Donald Jay and nose around Greater New York Crime Writers' headquarters on Sixth Avenue and Fifty-third Street. "I'm sorry I can't do more, Jake. I'm on deadline."

Modesty, though not happy about it, agreed to visit Carita Magenta on the pretext of having her aura aligned. She'd also try and get Wanda Sparks to arrange an interview with Rickie Romero.

"Since, apparently, Maurice and Venus are about to become an odd couple," Too Tall Tom said, "I'll talk to her, too."

That left me with my hero, Hunter Green; Dennis's new client, Ashley Butler; and, of course, the grieving widow, Edwina Carrington Fione. Plus three nagging puzzles. When and where had Charlie Fione and Holly

Halligan known each other? What was Hunter Green's relationship with Rickie Romero? Dennis had spotted the two of them having a confrontation in the men's room directly before Rickie and his fellow panelists had been served the cyanide. Even stranger, Hunter Green had acted as the literary liaison between Rickie and Wanda. Finally, Maurice Welch had purchased an Ashes Away package deal. Planning to sail into the sunset, then be flung into his final destination. How well had he known the cremation-cruise spokeswoman, Holly Halligan? Well enough to want her dead?

Crossing the street, heading home, I realized that I'd never even mentioned swing dancing to the ghosts.

Eight

There was no sign of Mom. And no note. My mother usually left chapter and verse detailing her comings and goings. This afternoon, she'd just left, without as much as an ETA for her homecoming. I'd turned off my cell phone, not wanting its ringing to disturb the Ghostwriters Anonymous meeting. Now I had three messages. Four, if I counted the one from the world beyond. Gypsy Rose's lengthy monologue had been recorded first.

"We should hold the séance as soon as possible. While I was meditating this morning, Zelda came through. She has a message for Dennis! From a sea captain who went down with his ship. And it's about Holly Halligan! Zelda flitted off—you know how she is—before I could get a clear signal, but something's up, up there! I thought perhaps we could combine a channeling with cocktails. How's this afternoon at five-thirty? At my place. Call me as soon as you receive this message. Dennis can make it and I'm asking Modesty,

too. And Jake, I've been trying to reach your mother. Where is she?"

How could anyone resist an invitation like that? And if Mom didn't return home in time to chat up Zelda Fitzgerald, it would serve her right for not letting anyone know where she'd gone. But I'd bet that wherever she was, Maura O'Hara's sixth sense would smell a séance.

I listened to my second message.

"Jake, it's Dennis. I've just finished reading one of the Ashes Away organization's files that Holly had left with me yesterday. It's labeled 'Assisted Crossings.' And it's going to make waves. I'm dropping the original off at Ben Rubin's office as soon as I hang up, but I've made a copy for you. I'll bring it along to Gypsy Rose's cocktails-with-the-dearly-departed party. Is she serving zombies? Maybe, after we're done with the dead, you and I can grab a few minutes alone."

As my heart thumped and my toes twitched, I couldn't decide which intrigued me more, the prospect of reading the Assisted Crossings file or the chance to spend some time alone with Dennis Kim.

The third message was from Hunter Green.

"Jake, I may have misled that homicide detective Ben Rubin. I know that he's a—er—a close friend of yours. And I know you're good at untangling the truth. Would you be kind enough to help me straighten out this mess before I'm in big trouble? Could we arrange to meet sometime this afternoon?"

How about that! My hero needed me, just when I needed to ask him a few questions. If there truly are no coincidences, this had to be a gift from the gods.

I promptly returned all three calls, confirming with Gypsy Rose, leaving a message for Dennis, and making a date with Hunter. Within fifteen minutes I'd brushed my teeth, combed my hair, reapplied my "Bare Bronze" lipstick, written a note for my mother—hey, one of us could act responsibly here—and was walking over to the Eighty-sixth Street subway station to catch a train downtown to Hunter Green's Tribeca loft.

On the corner of Park Avenue and Eighty-eighth Street, I ran into the Neals, my neighbors of twenty-five years. Slightly bent, he carried a cane and she clutched his arm. Marianne and Harry Neal had been married for over sixty years and the love light in their eyes had never dimmed. He'd retired as chair of philosophy at Columbia. Once she'd been a world-renowned William Butler Yeats scholar and had written several mysteries centered around her favorite poet. Nowadays she might forget her apartment number, but she could still quote Yeats with ease. Harry's mental agility seemed as acute as ever; Marianne's physical strength hadn't diminished very much. So today, they took care of each other with joy and patience. Setting a high standard. And making me wonder how one went from twitching toes to a lifetime of unconditional love.

When Mom had started working in the Corner Bookstore, then later at Gypsy Rose's, the Neals, who lived in a co-op on the first floor, were often my baby-sitters. Much of my love of literature had come from Marianne's reading aloud to me. And ever since my own Nana and Poppa had died years ago, I'd considered the Neals to be my surrogate grandparents. My mother and Gypsy Rose had them over for dinner at least once a week. Mr. Kim delivered their groceries and Dennis frequently drove them on their rounds to various doctors and medical labs.

This afternoon, based on their headgear, I guessed that they were still celebrating St. Patrick's Day. I'd never

seen a hat quite like Mrs. Neal's. Kelly green, with rib-
bons that tied under her chin, it somehow reminded me
of the bonnet that Rhett Butler had brought Scarlett
O'Hara back from Paris after the Civil War. Mr. Neal's
green plaid peaked cap was worn at a jaunty angle. Both
were quite dashing.

I kissed them, then blurted out Mom's engagement
announcement. Mrs. Neal smiled. "That's grand, dear."
Then she looked at her husband. "Will we still be here
for the wedding?" Mr. Neal patted her hand and changed
the subject.

"Jake, please tell your mother we'll be dropping by
soon to wish her well," Harry Neal said. "That Aaron
Rubin is one lucky man!"

I walked away, mulling over yet another puzzle.
What, if anything, had Marianne Neal's question about
her and her husband's future—or lack of same—meant?

. . . . .

If Andrew Carnegie's mansion had been
responsible for my uptown neighborhood's turn-of-the-
last-century cachet, then two factors that in the last
decade of the century had turned Tribeca trendy were
celebrity-owned restaurants and the stock market's
raging bulls.

Hunter Green lived in a converted warehouse with an
unimposing facade, a modest entrance hall, and a freight
elevator to his loft on the top floor. The elevator opened
into his amazing four thousand square feet of run-on
space, located under the highest cathedral ceiling and the
biggest skylight I've ever seen. Too Tall Tom's main
source of income came not from his ghosted, handyman-
how-to-books, but from his day job: turning New York
City's box-shape apartments into elegant Edwardian

flats. Some equally talented designer had transformed this formerly barren warehouse's top floor into an incredible loft.

I stood, savoring the oak beams and floor, Mission furniture, Pollock prints, and a color scheme Mom would have loved—a palette of neutrals ranging from cream to caramel. Totally drop-dead gorgeous. True crime must pay!

However, handsome Hunter, standing amidst all these clean lines and his beautiful possessions, looked uncomfortable.

"Coffee, Jake? Or would you like a drink?"

"No thanks, I've just come from brunch at Sarabeth's."

Hunter gave me a weak smile. "Best strawberry butter in the city." He ushered me to an Art Deco, crushed-velvet club chair, then sat on a matching love seat, facing me.

"Yes," I said, "but don't ever repeat that in front of Gypsy Rose. She's been trying to duplicate the recipe in her tearoom for years."

I didn't know Hunter Green very well, though I'd run into him at several Crime Writers events and had had this schoolgirl crush on him since—well, actually, since I'd been a schoolgirl. Once he'd recommended me, after a strong caveat, as a ghost for a Playboy bunny who'd wanted to write a police procedural. To no one's surprise, except for the bunny's, her book proposal never made it past the first pitch. With no hard feelings, she'd returned to her hutch, and I'd moved on to another murder. But Hunter had tried to help me. And, perhaps, that's all he'd done for Rickie Romero and Wanda Sparks: made another, more successful match between an "author" and a ghost.

Maybe now I could help him.

As if prompted by thought transference, he spoke. "You've developed a reputation as a pretty good amateur detective, and while I assume that your protagonists are, too—since you're a ghost, I can only guess what books you might have written—I'm referring to your real-life cases."

"What's wrong, Hunter?"

"I lied to Detective Rubin." Interesting. He'd moved from "misled" to "lied" in less than two hours.

"About what?"

"He asked how well I'd known Holly Halligan. I indicated that I'd met her through the Crime Writers' Conference. Because she'd been scheduled as a guest panelist." Hunter sighed. "But that wasn't entirely truthful."

"It wasn't?"

"No. As you know, my wife, Angela, died last year. I loved her deeply. She'd been ill for a long time. A slow and painful deterioration of her muscles. Anyway, someone had introduced Angela to Holly Halligan, and against my wishes, my wife purchased an Ashes Away burial at sea from her."

"Why wouldn't you want to tell Ben about that? He's bound to find out. And a cremation cruise isn't a crime. Well, not legally." I wondered if Hunter had been Angela's designated flinger.

"The voyage was a disaster." Hunter stared at his tented fingers. "I'd been so devastated during those last few weeks of Angela's illness that I'd left the planning up to Holly. Everything went wrong. My wife's remains arrived in a cardboard box, tied with string! The water had been rough, the stabilizer didn't seem to be working, and the boat rocked and rolled all the way out to deep water. Three of the four mourners were seasick. Holly had imported some L.A. charlatan to perform the ceremony. And Angela's ashes were scattered in the wrong direction. She'd always hated East Hampton." Tears filled Hunter's eyes. "By the time we'd docked, I could have killed Holly. Indeed, I mentioned that possibility, rather loudly, in front of the captain, the chaplain, and the few friends who'd sailed with us. But still, I don't know why I lied. Scared, I guess. You're right. For certain, Detective Rubin will discover the truth."

"Hunter, call Ben. Right now! Tell him everything, just the way you told me. He's a good guy. And it's better he hears this story from you."

"There's something else." Hunter rubbed his eyes.

I braced myself, realizing his next revelation might be much worse than the first. "And what would that be?"

"Well, as you may know, I sat in on Rickie Romero's trial. Great true-crime material. And later I interviewed him in jail. I even arranged for a—uh—an editor to help him with *Cat on Trump Tower's Roof*." I sympathized with Hunter. He couldn't reveal that Rickie Romero's best-seller had been ghosted by Wanda Sparks without breaking their—and his own—confidentiality. Though soon Hunter might have no choice.

Hunter stood, walked several yards over to a bar, and asked, "Are you sure you don't want a drink?"

I shook my head from side to side and waited silently while he poured himself a straight Johnny Walker Black. He returned to the love seat and continued, "All through his trial, Romero had sworn on his mother's grave that he hadn't stolen the cursed Faith diamond; so now that he's out, he can never sell it."

"Jeez! He really had stolen it?"

"During the course of our growing friendship, Rickie's veiled, but boastful, hints led me to figure out where he'd stashed the diamond. So you see, Jake, I also had a motive for attempting to murder him!"

Nine

The last owner of the Faith diamond had been another former MGM star, Susanne Tyler, whose seventh
husband, an Arabian emir, had given the fourteen-carat
gem to her as a wedding present. When Susanne had run
away with a plumber, she'd gotten custody of the diamond. Six months later the stone had vanished from her
East Coast residence, an eight-room apartment in the
Dakota on Central Park West. The police never figured
out how the thief had managed to break into the well-
fortified building, but they suspected that New York
City's most notorious cat burglar, Rickie Romero, had
been the culprit. However, with no witnesses, no prints,
and no DNA, the NYPD burglary squad couldn't prove
Romero had scored with the steal of the century. Neither
could the prosecutor at his trial, where Rickie had been
convicted of two other cat burglaries. And had become
something of a local folk hero in the process. A modern-
day Robin Hood, robbing the rich, but feeding Hell's
Kitchen's homeless.

I pondered all that jazz during the subway ride back uptown. Could Hell's Kitchen be the common denominator in this case? Senator Charlie Fione had grown up, as he often said in his campaign speeches, "on the sidewalks of New York," and those sidewalks were located in Hell's Kitchen. Since Romero had endowed a homeless shelter on Tenth Avenue, maybe, he'd grown up there, too. Of course, that would have been quite a few decades after the senator's childhood. Mom had told me that Holly Halligan had learned to ski as a child, in the mountains near her home, somewhere upstate, but could Holly have had a Hell's Kitchen connection?

Hunter Green neither told me how he'd stumbled onto the Faith diamond's hiding place nor where that location might be. After disclosing his multimillion-dollar motive, he'd seemed glad to see me go. However, he did say that Rickie Romero was well aware and really annoyed that Hunter had discovered where his cache was stashed.

Though at any moment Ben Rubin might soon change that status, Rickie Romero was a free man. If Rickie believed that Hunter had tried to poison him in order to sell the diamond, the cat burglar might decide to retaliate. Hunter Green might be in real danger. And not just from lying to Ben. Or could it be possible that my hero, Hunter, was the killer?

With three potential victims and a myriad of mixed motives, the murderer could be anyone who'd attended the Crime Writers' Conference. The leprechaun in the ladies' room had to be either the killer or his/her accomplice. I felt certain—well, almost certain—that either Wanda Sparks or Ashley Butler had dressed up as the little green man and served the pitcher of cyanide. And if neither had, one—or both of them—knew who did.

The train, a local, was packed. The disheveled young man, wrapped around the pole in front of me, alternated flirtatious glances in my direction with scratching what seemed to be a serious itch on his butt. A pretty kid, sloppily devouring a huge cone of cotton candy, sat to my right, and an enormous man, wearing too-tight exercise clothes, overlapped on my left. Every stop brought more hordes of people and more frustration into the subway car. By the time I breathed the fresh air, after a tight squeeze on the Ninety-sixth Street station's escalator, I had a double-strength headache.

I ran into my mother on the corner of Ninety-third and Madison, in front of Gypsy Rose's large, three-story red-brick house. Her bookstore/tearoom was located on the first floor.

Since Mom's tote bag always contained a mini medicine cabinet, as well as a large supply of tissues, cosmetics, hair and breath spray, and sundry snacks, I was able to swallow two Tylenol and wash them down with a small bottle of designer water. Maura O'Hara could have been the creator of the Boy Scouts motto.

"Where were you?" I asked.

"At Bloomingdale's." Her smile lit up the quickly darkening afternoon. "Checking out china patterns. I can't decide between Villeroy and Boch's Arco Weiss, with simple, almost stark, white lines, or a more elaborate, yet classic, Wedgwood design that evokes images of Jane Austen's England."

"What will you do with Nana's Wedgwood?"

"Why, I thought I'd give her dishes to you, darling. They are a family heirloom, and someday you can pass them on to your daughter."

I reached for another Tylenol.

My mother said, "That's too many!" But I swallowed it anyway.

Seemingly immune to my distress, my mother rattled on. "I stopped by the house, read your note, and called Gypsy Rose. Isn't it exciting? Zelda has a message for Dennis! Maybe your father sent one for me." She looked up at the sky. "I hope he'll give his blessing to my marriage." Then looked at me. "And I hope his daughter will give hers, too." I guess Mom wasn't immune after all.

Feeling scared, guilty, foolish, and loving, I put my arm around her shoulder. "I guess I don't want to lose you." Or my comfy co-op on Ninety-second Street.

"Lose me?" My mother sounded horrified. "Never! Did you know that the Ostertags' apartment on the third floor is up for sale? Aaron has suggested buying it and combining it with ours. Turning both apartments into one big duplex. You can have the top floor. And if you ever do get married, we can rethink the housing plan!"

As someone smarter than I once said: Be careful what you pray for, your prayers may be answered.

Modesty, her long, loose dress covered with a well-worn, ankle-length J. Peterman duster, bounced off the Madison Avenue bus and yelled from across the street, "Hey, Jake! I need to talk to you."

My mother touched my cheek. "Ben called. He'll be over around eight. Then the four of us will have dinner."

"The four of us?"

"Yes. A double date. Aaron and me and you and Ben. Just a little family postengagement party. I think Aaron plans on giving me a ring tonight."

Lord, were we going to celebrate every night until the wedding day? "Why don't you go ahead to Gypsy Rose's, Mom? I'll wait for Modesty."

Flushed a becoming shade of pink, Modesty arrived out of breath and agitated. "I've just returned from visiting Carita Magenta. She's the type of woman I really hate."

What woman wasn't? We ghosts have decided that with a few exceptions, Modesty has chosen to remain a misogynist, and has continued to work, exclusively, for women "authors" so that she can keep on bitching.

"Carita's so smug in that colorful New Age cocoon of hers that she's rude as—well, much ruder—than I could ever be."

"Don't sell yourself short, Modesty. Now tell me what happened. Where, exactly, is Carita's cocoon?"

"In Murray Hill. On First Avenue, right across the street from the morgue. It's a refurbished tenement, but Carita still has the bathtub in the kitchen. She painted it purple; the kitchen itself is hot orange, with chartreuse floorboards and molding. And when I arrived, I found Venus DeMill sitting in the tub, up to her neck in bubbles, downing a huge manhattan."

I laughed.

"It isn't funny, Jake." Nothing ever was to Modesty. "They'd both had far too many manhattans and Carita was totally out of line. What a foul mouth that big broad has! Incidentally, she'd never fit in that tiny tub. I guess during the Great Depression, people were smaller. Anyway, Venus DeMill's legs were dangling almost to the floor. She paints her toenails bright yellow. Carita says that's because Venus has an aura of sunshine."

"Come on, Modesty, we'll be late for the séance!" We walked toward the bookstore's entrance, on Ninety-third, just steps off Madison.

"But listen, Jake! Carita claimed to have been robbed by Rickie Romero! Said it was a colorful, almost mystical experience! Said Rickie's aura is apricot. And all the while Venus kept yelling at Carita, trying to get her to shut up."

"What! When did this robbery occur?"

"Years ago. But Carita sounded furious that the entire episode, though thinly veiled, had been exposed in what she referred to as one of *Cat on Trump Tower's Roof*'s more intriguing chapters."

"Jeez! What else did Carita say?"

"Nothing." Modesty shuddered. "Venus rose from the tub and strongly suggested that I leave."

"What did you do?"

"What do mean what did I do? I got the hell out of there!"

"Modesty, run in and tell Mom and Gypsy Rose that I'll be right there."

"Where are you going?"

"Gypsy Rose only carries self-help and New Age stuff. I want to see if the Corner Bookstore still has a copy of *Cat on Trump Tower's Roof*. Mom lent hers to Mr. Kim."

"You plan on reading it during the séance?"

I ignored her and dashed across the street.

A huge clap of thunder accompanied my purchase of Rickie Romero's best-seller. By the time I signed the charge slip, rain was pummeling the avenue. I asked the saleslady for an extra plastic bag, tied it over my hair, stuffed my package under my jacket, stepped outside to brave the elements, and quite literally bumped into the book's author.

"You're that pretty lady from the Crime Writer's Conference." Rickie's smile dazzled, even as the rain pelted my face. "The one who said that all three of us had been poisoned."

"Yeah, well, I'm glad I was wrong." I brushed the water from my eyes as the wind blew the plastic bag off my head and carried it into the gutter. Reaching under my jacket, I extracted my package and said, "I've just bought a copy of your book. In fact, I plan to read it— cover to cover—tonight."

"Do you live in the neighborhood?"

"Right around the corner. On Ninety-second Street."

"I'm staying at a friend's house over on Fifth." Rickie gestured toward the west. "This is transition time for me. A period of adjustment between jail and my own apartment. Though I'm kind of worried." His sooty eyelashes were so thick that the raindrops landing there served to weigh them down. "I think that homicide detective Ben Rubin would like my next move to be back into a cell."

I didn't have a clue about how to respond to that.

Rickie bent down and brushed my windswept hair out of my eyes. "Perhaps you'd be kind enough to meet me for brunch and a book review tomorrow?"

The cat burglar and I arranged a Sunday-morning date. Then, soaking wet but feeling sixteen, I finally headed to the séance.

Ten

They'd gathered around the table when I arrived. Mom sat between Gypsy Rose and Modesty. Dennis sat to my favorite psychic's left. Apologizing for holding things up, I took the chair next to him. Gypsy Rose's séances were casual affairs. Just family and a few close friends channeling their dead loved ones. Frankly, the results could be hit-or-miss, as the lines of communication weren't always open. Or, if open, none too clear. Sometimes, the channels seemed clogged. Full of nasty, squawky noise. But no conversation. No thought transference. No field reports from any plane. Then Gypsy Rose's complaints of static would remind me of those old Sprint commercials. Sometimes, the call just didn't go through. Other times, chatting up the spirit guides, who acted as conduits to the world beyond, worked wonderfully well. And, on occasion, Gypsy Rose would score a direct connection to the soul in question.

Gypsy Rose's town house had been built less than a decade after Andrew Carnegie's mansion, making it one of the oldest homes in the neighborhood. Solid red brick, with several working fireplaces, well-polished oak floors, and filled with lovingly selected furnishings spanning several eras, the house had a lived-in look, both comforting and charming. Like its owner. Today's channeling was being conducted in her second-floor library. A great room, with twelve-foot-high ceilings and walls lined with cherry bookcases, spread across the entire length of the house.

I'm convinced if Gypsy Rose hadn't been a psychic and an entrepreneur, she could have had a career as an interior designer. When Louie Liebowitz had died, leaving behind a widow still in her early thirties—Mom always said, "Just like Jackie Kennedy!"—Gypsy Rose had reinvented herself as our neighborhood's favorite fortune-teller. She'd parlayed a small inheritance, a knack for cards—she could have beaten Bill Clinton at hearts—and an interest in New Age phenomena into a thriving business. With a bookstore/tearoom that promoted ESP and writers who specialized in reincarnation, spirit guides, angels, and aliens, she'd turned alternative-lifestyle authors into celebrities. And, in the process, had become one of Carnegie Hill's most successful and well-known women.

Mom and Gypsy Rose were closer than sisters, and I had benefited from their relationship. Having no children and being naturally generous and loving, Gypsy Rose had showered attention and affection on me for over twenty-five years. Like Mom, I adored her. As far as these intimate hookups with the world beyond went, I reserved judgment, but often wondered: How the hell were we receiving messages from Zelda Fitzgerald? Yet I believed that Gypsy Rose believed. And some totally unexplainable, strange stuff had gone down during previous channelings that I'd attended. I'd even had a chat with Emily Brontë or some other nonblithe spirit doing a damn good imitation of Emily. So, I've kept an open mind.

Dennis, on the other hand, remained a total skeptic. Only his good breeding and fear of his father's wrath and/or of hurting Mom and Gypsy Rose, combined with curiosity, had kept his mouth shut at these séances. But even Dennis had admitted to being impressed with Gypsy Rose's contacts. And what she'd gleaned from them. On whatever plane where they might be hanging out.

Gypsy Rose has a sunshine policy for séances. Lights on. Eyes wide open. No hidden props, mysterious rappings, creaking doors, smoke, or mirrors. The living don't hold hands or meditate. The dead don't levitate. And Gypsy Rose has encouraged us to keep talking as she opens communications with the world beyond. "The spirits like to keep things lively!" Sometimes she used a Ouija board, but since there wasn't one on the table, I gathered this afternoon would be a no-frills quickie.

I dried my hair with the embroidered tea towel that Gypsy Rose had handed me, then wrapped it, turban style, around my head as she laid out the séance's sequence. "Okay, I'm going to channel Zelda. As you all know, I'll be in a trance and she'll use my body. With any luck, she'll show up. This *was* her idea. Zelda asked to speak to Dennis, so chances are she'll take a few minutes out of her postlife partying to visit with us."

"I thought we were going to contact Holly Halligan," Modesty said.

Gypsy Rose said, "That's right. But this message comes from a sea captain who went down with his ship, and it concerns Holly Halligan. After we hear it, I'll have Zelda channel Holly's spirit guide."

"Maybe this captain will turn out to *be* her guide!" my mother said. "Holly really loved the ocean."

Modesty snarled, "She'd sunk to the bottom, selling the sea as a cemetery."

Dennis laughed. "Yeah. But that huckster bought into her own pitch. Would you like to guess who's been assigned as keeper of her urn? Damn nuisance. I have to deliver it to Norway, after stopping in Paris to pick up Jean-Claude, the designated flinger, for her Ashes Away cruise through the fjords. Holly's ship-shaped-like-a-ski isn't finished yet. So I guess I'll have to stow her in my office until it's christened. The Staten Island Ferry would have been a hell of a lot more convenient." At my mother's frown, he added, "Er—no disrespect intended, Maura!"

"Are you her executor?" I asked.

"Not a role an entertainment lawyer usually gets to play." Dennis shrugged. "But yes, I am, as of two days ago. Little did I know I'd be on call so soon."

"Another soul's ashes are a big responsibility," Modesty said. "Lillian Hellman served as Dorothy Parker's executrix, but she left Dottie's urn with her attorney, and the ashes remained in his office safe for decades. That's another reason why I'm going directly to the grave in one piece."

I wondered who'd inherit Holly's estate—probably a very large treasure chest. When Dennis and I had our meeting after the séance, I'd try and pry that information out of him.

"Is there anyone here?" a refined, slightly southern voice inquired, sounding more amused than annoyed. Gypsy Rose had gone and Zelda had arrived. And we'd all been so busy gabbing, no one had even noticed.

"Yes!" I said. "This is Jake O'Hara speaking, Zelda. You have a message for Dennis Kim?" I gestured toward him.

"Hello there, Jake! Your father speaks so often and so fondly of you that I feel as if I'm part of the family. Actually, I did know you once in Paris." As I was about to ask her if we'd been fellow expatriates, she continued. "But that was then and this is now. And I've come to deliver an important message."

"From a sea captain?" I asked, hoping I could catch up on my previous life with Zelda at another time.

"Indeed. A Captain Smith. He went down with his ship. The *Titanic*. Its sinking in 1912 caused quite a stir when I was a girl. God, almost a century ago!" Zelda sighed. "Anyway, he's spending eternity in a most agitated state. A real wet blanket. His message seems muddled, but perhaps you all can make sense out of it: 'Some crossings aren't aboveboard.' The captain told me that it came from a recent arrival in the world beyond, Holly Halligan."

"That's it?" Modesty said.

Dennis asked Zelda, "What does that mean?" I knew he hated talking to a spirit.

"I deliver; I don't decipher. I told you the captain's not on an even keel. Always complaining about the cold. And ice, can't even mention it! Ice is a dirty word to Captain Smith. Sorry, I have to toddle off. Eugene O'Neill is on another plane, doing another one of his dreary readings, and the Murphys will kill me—well, it's too late for that, but you know what I mean—if I don't show up!"

"Wait!" I yelled. "Is Captain Smith Holly Halligan's spirit guide?"

"No, Sonny Bono is her guide. Skiing gave them common ground. As did living in California. And, of course, they were both performers, weren't they?" Zelda, using Gypsy Rose's features, smirked. "I must go! Sonny's at the House of Representatives tax hearing. Some spirits just can't let go of their past lives. But wait . . . you all are in luck, here's Holly herself!"

"Dennis! Are you there?" Though she was using Gypsy Rose's voice, there was no mistaking Holly Halligan's tone.

"Present!" Dennis jumped up.

"Who killed us?" Holly almost wailed. "I can't locate Charlie Fione; he must be on a different plane. And there's no record of Rickie Romero ever arriving here. Who wanted us all dead? You must avenge these murders, Dennis. As my attorney and my executor. What is my estate paying you for, if not to find my killer?"

"Can't you give us a clue?" he asked, squirming in his seat and sounding totally uncomfortable.

"Just don't smear my memory, Dennis. The answers may be in the Assisted Crossings folder. Some Ashes Away passengers had more help than others, if you get my drift. And certainly, check out Edwina Carrington. If ever a woman had a motive for murder, she did. Maurice Welch, too. I once had a brief encounter . . . well, never mind. One more thing. My ashes. Don't leave them alone on a shelf. Not even for a minute. I've always loved running loose around New York. Carry my urn with you, Dennis. At all times. Everywhere you go. Until you board the ski-shape ship for my final voyage. Or I'll haunt you for the rest of your lives. Now this séance is history. Get to work."

Then, just as suddenly as she'd arrived, Holly Halligan departed and Gypsy Rose returned, asking, "What happened?" But the rest of us were speechless.

Eleven

Modesty had a mysterious early-Saturday-evening date of her own, but it wasn't easy getting away from Mom and Gypsy Rose. I finally resorted to Dennis's favorite confidentiality excuse, claiming that he and I had ghostwriting business to discuss. In private.

Though my hair had dried, my head now looked like a bowl of fuzzy noodles. Fortunately, the soft lighting in the Stanhope's bar covered a multitude of sins. Our corner table was so tiny that Dennis's leg was locked against mine. The forced intimacy felt good. He'd been unusually quiet, almost reflective, since we'd left Gypsy Rose's and he'd scoured the streets until we'd found a legal parking space. The spirits seemed to have spooked him.

We ordered martinis and I toyed with the mixed nuts. You'd think the Stanhope Hotel's management could divest itself of a few peanuts considering the cost of their cocktails, and worse, why had they turned the lounge into a cigar bar? Dennis remained silent. I pictured that logical, lawyerly mind of his reeling in turmoil. Dealing with Zelda had left me feeling discombobulated, too. And Holly Halligan had proved to be more difficult dead than she had been alive.

I'd wait till the drinks arrived, and if he hadn't come back down to earth by then, I'd ask to see the Assisted Crossings file. It wasn't as if we had all night here. Thanks to my mother, I had a double date for dinner and I wanted to wash my hair. Yet even with Dennis's deepening silence, I felt comfortable—almost cozy—sitting so close to him. His leg next to my thigh. His mind God only knows where. Maybe words were our enemy.

The waiter placed a crystal glass in front of me. I raised it. "To us . . . working together to find Holly's killer!"

Dennis said, "I can't drink to that."

"Why not? Your client's spirit just made that request quite clear."

"Holly or Gypsy Rose—or whatever weirdo controlled that channeling—didn't know I'd already gone through that file." The folder in question lay teasingly between us on the table. "I don't know why I ever told you about it. In this case, knowledge could be dangerous. And with all the motives in that file, I don't want to be responsible for the killer coming after you."

I clutched the folder to my breast and stood up. "I absolve you of all blame in the unlikely event of my murder. Now, can we talk or do I have to steal this and make a quick getaway? I'll bet that after all these years I can still run faster than you!"

"Sit down, Nancy Drew." Dennis smiled up at me. "I know I'm going to regret this. Maybe not now, but soon, and for the rest of my life."

"You never could get that *Casablanca* quote quite

right." I sat and picked up my glass again. "Here's looking at you, kid." Then I opened the file.

Ten minutes later suspects and their motives were spread across the table. Holly Halligan had not only represented Ashes Away, she'd been the company's largest stockholder and chairman of the board. In addition to arranging complete cremation burial-at-sea cruises, including the urn, a customized memorial ceremony, and a final fling aboard a ship priced to accommodate the deceased's—or the bereaved's—budget, Ashes Away could, upon request, provide an additional service. Holly's profitable sideline had been helping the grim reaper to arrive early. She'd introduce those future passengers who had purchased her packages but were suffering from the pain of "a long bon voyage" to Dr. Anna Nujurian. The good doctor, currently out on bail while awaiting trial for assisted suicide in Westchester County, had oozed empathy and kindly provided prescriptions to send those poor souls on a speedy last trip. "Sailing to their last port of call . . . Heaven!" Holly reported in her extensive logs of previous Ashes Away assisted crossings.

The waiter appeared. I declined a second drink; Dennis ordered another martini.

Angela Green had been among the passengers whom Holly had helped to heaven. She'd met with Dr. Nujurian without her husband's knowledge. Hunter had found out about the assisted suicide aboard the boat, on the day of his wife's funeral, when Holly presented him with an itemized bill. God! So that, not the tacky funeral service, had been the real reason Hunter had threatened Holly in front of all the mourners. A major motive! Then, too, he had that multimillion-dollar motive for murdering Rickie Romero—the Faith diamond.

And Senator Fione had been scheduled to see Dr. Nu-jurian next Tuesday. "Jesus! Your father was right, Dennis. Charlie Fione actually did have an appointment with Death, but his murder canceled it!"

"Read on, Jake. It looks as if Edwina made all the arrangements. I wonder if Charlie ever knew he'd been booked on an Ashes Away cruise, or that he had a date to discuss his quality of death with Dr. Assisted Suicide."

"He must have known! But maybe when Edwina told Charlie about the plans, he balked. And maybe she mixed up a batch of cyanide to move up his estimated time of departure!"

"Sounds like a plot to me." Dennis frowned. "But then who is the leprechaun? She or he must have been working with Edwina. Or whoever poisoned the panel."

"So it would seem." Dennis damn well had to be aware that his newest client, Ashley Butler, along with Wanda Sparks, was a prime candidate for the little-green-man role.

I closed the file. None of the other six assisted crossings had lived in or near Manhattan or had been writers. While one of their surviving relatives might have had a motive for killing Holly Halligan, he/she probably wouldn't have had means or opportunity to kill at the conference. Unless said survivor was also a member of the Greater New York Crime Writers' Association. Ben Rubin, no doubt, was investigating all this information right now. That task would be enormous. I'd bet he'd be a no-show, again, at dinner. And if I didn't get moving, I wouldn't make it either. Which was okay with me.

Dennis smiled and reached for my hand. "Even with your macaroni-salad hairdo and the unpleasant topic under discussion, it's a delight to be with you, Jake."

Jesus! Could he be drunk? "Yeah. Well, I do appreciate your sharing this file with me. This mystery is making me crazy. So many crosscurrents . . ."

"Listen, could we talk about our own crosscurrents for a change? For twenty-five years we've been like ships passing in the night." He squeezed my fingers, and his touch, as always, traveled like lightning down to my toes. As a woman who considered herself to be a sassy, smart, sophisticated New York ghost, I now agonized over my loss of words. Finally, I settled for a nod. Then to my own and, I'm sure, Dennis's amazement, I leaned across the table and kissed him on the lips. A chaste kiss, to be sure, but my free hand stroked his leg that was still locked against mine.

Then, embarrassed by my boldness, I fumbled for the folder. "This only contains a list of those passengers who'd purchased the services of Dr. Nujurian. But Maurice Welch bought an Ashes Away cruise, too. I wonder what went on between him and Holly. And I'd like to know if any of the other suspects had planned on having a burial at sea."

Dennis laughed. "Okay, back to murder. But when this case is closed, you and I are going to have an open discussion. Not from different ships, but with our feet firmly planted on the sidewalks of New York. I want you to promise me we'll have that talk."

I felt the color rush to my cheeks. "I—er—I promise, Dennis." He kissed me on top of my tangled head.

As he signaled for the check, I said, "There's one more thing I'd like to know. Who inherits Holly's estate?"

"I've been waiting all afternoon for that question." Dennis grinned. "You know that's one discussion I shouldn't be having with you. Maybe you can charm homicide's finest, Ben Rubin, into telling you."

"When the will goes into probate, won't it become public knowledge anyway? Come on, Dennis!"

"Yes, it will." Dennis signed the credit card. I waited. "Oh hell, it's bound to leak even sooner than that. And I'd so enjoy seeing the expression on your face when you find out—"

"Tell me!" I shouted, eliciting a disapproving look from the dowager seated at the table to our right.

"Holly Halligan's entire estate, including Ashes Away, and totaling over twenty million dollars, goes to her sole heir . . ." Dennis drummed his knuckles on the table. "Da-da-dee-dum . . ."

"Who?"

As she addressed her elderly male companion, the dowager's upper-crust voice carried to our table. "I can remember when the cocktail hour at the Stanhope was sacrosanct. Noise was minimal. Good manners prevailed."

Ignoring her, I said, *"Who,* Dennis? Who is it?"

"Rickie Romero, that's who!"

Seriously regretting that I hadn't ordered a second martini, I reached over and drained Dennis's.

Twelve

I arrived home in a frenzy, wondering how I could shower, blow-dry my hair, and get dressed in ten minutes. Not to mention makeup. Even for a low-maintenance-toilette type, who'd be willing to challenge her personal best time, that would be an impossible task. But I need not have worried. Both my mother and I had been stood up.

"First Ben called and canceled." My mother, her eyes fully lined, shadowed, and coated with mascara, but without lipstick, and wearing her old terrycloth beach robe and blue fuzzy mules that should have been thrown out a decade ago, obviously had been interrupted in the middle of putting on her face. "You know how close-mouthed Ben can be; he's such a just-the-facts-ma'am guy, isn't he? But something was up. Anyway, I'd no sooner hung up when Aaron called. He proved to be a tad more forthcoming."

I was sorry that I'd missed Mom's telephone inquisition. Of course, poor Aaron had talked. He'd been up against Carnegie Hill's only KGB agent. "So what did he have to say?"

"It looks as if they're ready to arrest Hunter Green! He had two strong motives. Threatening Holly Halligan in front of witnesses, for God's sake. And another for killing Rickie Romero. Aaron didn't say what that motive was, but I'll bet it had something to do with the Faith diamond! I remember that flap over the Faith from the trial." Mom was a Court TV junkie. And one smart cookie. "But I'll never believe that Hunter is capable of murder. No matter how many motives he might have had! Gypsy Rose is heartsick. She's trying to contact Angela as we speak!"

"Where is Aaron now?"

"He's gone over to the precinct to help Ben go through some file. Aaron said in an investigation like this, with three high-profile intended victims—Romero's surviving only complicates the case—narrowing down which one had been the real target is an overwhelming job! And if the killer wanted two—or all three—of them dead, the case becomes even crazier. The homicide department's short on manpower. All the available detectives are out detecting. So Aaron will work the phones, calling in a few favors from his district-attorney days."

"Did he mention if the police have discovered who dressed up as the leprechaun?" The police knew Rickie was Holly's heir. And Wanda had been Rickie's ghost. More than a ghost.

"No. They haven't." My mother sighed. "Strange that you should ask that, dear. Aaron did say that they'd found the costume. Green tunic and tights, black boots, a green hat, and gloves. They'd been stuffed inside the Modess dispenser. The police had overlooked it during their initial search. And it wasn't until today, when a woman complained to the Plaza management that the dispenser was jammed, that the clothes were found."

"Hmmph. There you go! I'd just bet that those cops who searched the ladies' room were all men. That's why they ignored the Modess machine. And I'd also bet it was a woman who stashed the costume there."

My mother smiled. "I'd back that bet. But remember your promise: don't start snooping. I have enough to worry about. Though I do think we should talk to Ben. We probably can't reach him tonight, but first thing to-morrow! Hunter's no killer!"

"I'll call Ben in the morning," I said, thinking that Detective Rubin would be thrilled to hear how much Mom and I disapproved of his conclusions in this case.

"Well, now that we've been dumped in favor of detective work, what about dinner? Can I interest you in a pizza and a video? Maybe a murder mystery? I'll even go get them."

"Not in that outfit, I hope. Okay, I'll hop in the shower and be ready for show time when you return. We'll watch the movie while we eat, but then I'm going to bed with a book that I have to read tonight."

"Hitchcock?" my mother asked as she started toward her bedroom.

"Yeah. That's perfect. Rent *To Catch a Thief*."

But the best-laid plans of mothers and daughters, as well as of mice and men, do ofttimes go astray.

The phone started ringing as soon as I'd stepped into the shower and soaped up my hair. It continued ringing on and off through the creme rinse. Finally, wrapped in a towel, but still dripping, I answered it.

"Jake, I have to see you right now!" Modesty shouted.

"I'm all wet. What's up?"

"Wanda Sparks. She called me about an hour ago,

wanting to talk to me about the program. As you know, I agreed to be her sponsor. She's in a real anonymity crisis. Can't cope with her lack of identity. And Jake"— Modesty lowered her voice to a whisper—"you won't believe the stuff she's spilling. I think we have at least two more motives for murder here. And possibly a third. Wanda herself could be our killer. Furthermore, we're stuck on step one. Wanda's in big-time denial." Modesty had returned to shouting. "I need your support as a sister member of Ghostwriters Anonymous. Now get over here!"

Modesty's "over here" turned out to a less-than-desirable area. Located on a side street, two avenues away from the Hudson River in the northwest end of Chelsea, Wanda Sparks's small apartment building was beyond bleak. An aging, limestone tenement with dingy windows, its facade had never faced a steam blast.

The damp cold air pierced through my parka and I shivered as I tried to find Wanda's bell in the dim light trickling down from a sixty-watt bulb located in an old rusty fixture high above the front door.

I'd done some fast talking and faster eating when my mother had returned with the pizza. She'd accused me of reprising my Nancy Drew routine and I hadn't even tried to deny it. When I assured her that I was only going to meet Modesty and Wanda Sparks—avoiding any mention of an address—and Wanda might have some information that could clear Hunter, Mom simmered down. "It won't be the first time I've watched *To Catch a Thief* alone."

That had to be the understatement of the new century. Over the years, to my certain knowledge, Mom has watched that flick—all alone—at least fifty times. And dozens of other times in the company of her darling daughter. Just last week she'd roped Aaron into viewing it with her.

"Good. You and Grace can seduce Cary one more time."

"Don't be late. I'm waiting up." Then she insisted that I leave Wanda's phone number. She read it and frowned. "Where is this prefix? I hope you're not traveling to a bad neighborhood. You and Modesty be sure and take a cab home."

She'd be delighted to learn that I'd decided to follow her advice. If cabs cruised this block that late at night.

Straining my eyes—God, I hoped I didn't need glasses—I finally found Wanda's apartment number and pressed the bell. A shrill buzzer signaled that the door could now be opened. I walked into a dark foyer filled with the scent of stale brussels sprouts.

Wanda lived on the fifth floor. No elevator. Climbing the stairs, I thought this had better be good. If Modesty had dragged me "over here" for anything less than information leading to the discovery of the real suspect, who then could replace Hunter in that role, I'd never share another Sarabeth muffin with her again.

Modesty opened the door. The studio, less than five hundred square feet, turned out to be quite charming Like a college dorm decorated by Ralph Lauren. A sleigh bed against the wall to my left, covered in a dark green-and-navy plaid, with matching puffy pillows and duvet, doubled as a couch. Two tall bookcases, crammed with murder mysteries, stood on either side of the bed. The other walls were covered with theater posters, mostly from forty's musicals. An oval oak table and four ladder-back chairs with cushions covered in the same fabric as the sleigh bed were placed in front of three windows that the morning sun would stream through.

Wanda sat in one of those chairs, holding her cheeks with both hands. I noticed a coffee pot and a pound cake on the table. Good. At least I could eat. Three closed, attractive white enamel louver doors led, I presumed, to a kitchenette, a bathroom, and a closet. And, in one corner of the room, Wanda had set up a tidy and efficient mini-office. Straight from the Hold Everything catalog.

Modesty and I joined a now-weeping Wanda at the table. I reached for the cake. "Okay, how can I help?"

"Wanda's feeling rage for Rickie Romero," Modesty said as she poured the coffee. "She'd like to kill him for not giving her any credit—not even 'as told to'—for writing most of *Cat on Trump Tower's Roof*."

Thinking that maybe she *had* tried to poison him, but only succeeded in killing two other innocent people—boy, that might lead to real rage—I said, "Having been a ghost for ten years, I certainly can empathize with those feelings." I was not only identifying with the newest member of Ghostwriters Anonymous, I might be unmasking a murderer. Jane would be appalled. I felt a wave of guilt. My words sounded so sincere, but my motives were not exactly in the spirit of the program's principles. Yet I plunged right on. "How much of the book did you write?"

Wanda took a sip of coffee. "At least half. And, I edited. Then I rewrote the whole damn thing. Rickie had a concept and characters. I developed the thread that held the segments together and provided the needle that sewed the plot together. He'd still be stuck in Chapter Two!" Tears streamed down her cheeks.

I handed her a napkin. "Give me an example. Say, the chapter about Carita Magenta. I know the names have been changed, but did you or Rickie write that one?" My mother's brief book review of *Cat on Trump*

Tower's Roof had given me no hint of what might have infuriated Carita. Yet Magenta had told Modesty that Rickie had maligned her. Maybe I would hear the story from the ghostwriter's mouth.

"Rickie wrote the first draft of that one." Wanda sobbed and blew her nose in the napkin. I handed her another one. "I rewrote. And it turned out to be one of the more intriguing chapters in the book!"

Modesty caught my eye. Strange, Wanda just used the exact same words that Carita Magenta had used when describing the chapter to Modesty. I asked Wanda, "Why do you say that?"

"It's the hottest chapter in the book. That's why," Wanda said. "Well, except for one where the cat burglar crawls naked into that palace in Venice and steals an emerald necklace and the princess's heart." If it meant staying up all night, I had to read this book. "Anyway, in the chapter based on the Carita Magenta robbery, the thief spies on two wild women cavorting in bed. Then the three of them sit around and, over drinks, discuss how aura can color sex, before he takes off with the jewels. Both the female characters are famous writers, thinly disguised versions of Carita Magenta and Venus DeMill."

How had my mother missed that? Since Venus, the literary world's sex symbol, had just announced her engagement to that same world's macho drunk, Maurice Welch, and since Rickie Romero had been scheduled for a cross-country book tour, giving dozens of television interviews, I could smell two or three more motives for murder. I cut another slice of pound cake.

"Anonymity isn't Wanda's only problem," Modesty prompted. "She's stressed-out big time working for Donald Jay."

I refilled Wanda's cup. "Before we talk about Donald Jay, how about some cake? It's great. Where did you buy it?"

She almost smiled. "I made it. Rickie's favorite recipe. I must have brought a dozen or more of these pound cakes to him in prison. Maybe I will have a smidgen."

"What's wrong at Crime Writers?" I asked. Then added, "I do think Donald Jay is the prizewinning jerk of the Western world."

"And the meanest bastard in Manhattan." Wanda shoved her fork into the pound cake, sending crumbs flying across the table. She jumped from her chair, grabbed a napkin, and began to wipe them up. "Nothing I do is ever right. Though he's just as rotten to Ashley Butler and the rest of the staff. And, for the most part, they're volunteers. Wannabe writers. Treats them like dirt. But as the paid help, Ashley and I take the brunt of his abuse."

I felt sorry for her. And ashamed about picking her befuddled brain. "You have enough to deal with during these early stages of recovery. Learning how to cope with your anonymity is your most important assignment right now! Isn't that right, Modesty? Maybe it will help you if we share our experiences about working with wicked bosses."

"It might," Wanda said. "But Donald Jay is more than a wicked man. I think he might have killed Senator Fione. And Holly Halligan as well, just because she happened to be there. Rickie Romero would be dead, too, if he'd still been drinking."

"Was that common knowledge?" I asked. "I mean, like, were you, for example, aware that Rickie never drank?"

Wanda hesitated before answering. "Well—er—not

really. That topic never came up during our conversations in his prison cell. When he got out, I noticed that he never ordered wine with dinner, but I didn't ask why."

Right! I nodded. "Just curious. Now, why would Donald Jay want to kill Charlie Fione?"

"Something to do with the Senate's upcoming bill concerning the federal government's Waste Management Project. Because Donald Jay owns the land in Plattsburgh—that's up near Canada, you know—where they were planning on building a huge new facility. Donald would have made big bucks and he's broke. An assistant overhears a lot of garbage. Anyway, the senator wanted to scratch the whole deal. It would have been close, but Fione, probably, could have gotten enough votes to squash the project. Donald screamed at him on the phone Friday afternoon. Said the senator would put him in the poorhouse. And the vote was to have been held this coming Monday. Of course, now the Senate has shut down its chambers until after Charlie Fione's funeral."

I would have settled for only one more motive. Modesty had thought we'd have three. Now there were four. Carita Magenta, Venus DeMill, Maurice Welch, and Donald Jay. Make that five. Wanda Sparks had motive, means, and opportunity. She certainly could have been the leprechaun carrying that pitcher of poisoned beer to Rickie Romero and she could have been working alone.

Thirteen

I woke up grumpy. Six hours doesn't do it for me. Reading Rickie Romero's roman à clef until three A.M. had been intriguing, though somewhat less than informative, and certainly not worth the sleep-deprived crankiness that I was suffering from as I reached for the bedside phone. The grandmother clock in the foyer chimed nine times. Damn! Ben Rubin would be tough to reach at this hour, and I really wanted to discuss those five other motives with him. After trying him at homicide, home, and on his cell phone, and reciting the same message three times—"It's urgent that we speak ASAP"—I could only hope that he'd reach me before I had to leave for my book-review brunch with Rickie.

Modesty and I had shared a midnight ride in a gypsy cab and rehashed the case on our way uptown. I told her that Hunter Green had become the police's number-one choice for double murderer. Since the evening had unearthed several other killer candidates, we decided that I should share that information with Ben, pronto. And try to get Hunter off the hot seat. The trick would be convincing Ben that Modesty and I had somehow stumbled upon these suspects and that I hadn't been playing Nancy Drew. Or giving Modesty her well-deserved credit in this case, Holmes and Watson.

Mom scurried around the apartment, overscrambling eggs and setting bagels afire in the toaster oven while attempting to get ready for mass at St. Thomas More's. True to her threat, she'd been wide-awake when I'd arrived home last night, torn between approval of my attempts to clear Hunter and dismay that my detective work might put me in danger. This morning, as she smeared cream cheese on a cinnamon-raisin bagel, she said, "You can't trust that Wanda woman; she could be the killer, herself, and just trying to incriminate the others."

"I know, Mom, but if we can convince Ben that someone else, possibly even Wanda, may be our murderer, Hunter might be off the hook. Last night you were urging me to call Ben!"

"Look, I like and respect Hunter Green and I'm certain he's innocent; however, my main concern is for you. Tell Ben all you know, then drop the digging. Whoever poisoned Holly Halligan and Charlie Fione is a cold-blooded, bold, premeditated killer. I don't want you to become his or her next victim." Then, as she poured my tea, she added, "And don't accept anything to drink from anyone!"

When I laughed, she drank it herself. I poured another cup and brought it, my bagel, and The *New York Times* back to bed. The deaths by poisoning of Holly Halligan and Charlie Fione had made the headlines for the second day in a row. How those two old hams would have enjoyed seeing themselves on the front page. Great photos of both of them. Holly's on skis, reproduced from a fifties movie still glossy, and Charlie's snapped on the floor of the Senate during the impeachment vote. I wondered if the souls in the world beyond had access to newspapers. Maybe Gypsy Rose could ask Zelda Fitzgerald. My father used to read me the comics in the *Daily News* every day. And he'd loved politics and sports. Did Dad know today's scores? Maybe I could bring these clippings to the next channeling and ask their spirit guides to read them to Holly and Charlie. Then again, maybe I'd become as flaky as dandruff.

I took a bite from my too-toasted bagel and turned to the story's follow-up pages. Some sob sister had written a lengthy human-interest background piece on Charlie Fione's impoverished Hell's Kitchen childhood. He'd lived in a tenement on Tenth Avenue between Forty-ninth and Fiftieth. Poor on a poor block in a poor neighborhood. And a tough one. Lots of gangsters had come out of Hell's Kitchen, but senators stepping up from its streets were scarcer than debutantes.

Charlie's mother had been widowed when her husband, a twenty-five-year-old longshoreman, had been crushed on the Hudson River docks when a crate, lowered from the *Queen Mary*, had slipped loose from its ropes. Maria Fione had been left with three children, the oldest six, no family in America, and zero income or pension. Working two jobs, the young woman had managed to educate her two young sons and daughter. Mrs. Fione had lived with her daughter and son-in-law in Scarsdale until she'd died in 1985. Charlie's older brother had become a priest, and currently was serving as pastor of Sacred Heart, the church and grade school that all three of the Fione children had attended. Their baby sister, now known as Fatima Fione-Epstein, taught English Lit. at Columbia.

While the funeral plans were not yet firm, Father Joseph Fione had indicated to the *Times* reporter that together with the cardinal of the City of New York, he would be celebrating the Mass of Requiem for his dead brother at St. Patrick's Cathedral. And that joining the speaker of the House, the senior senator from Massachusetts, and the mayor of New York, Professor Fatima Fione-Epstein would be delivering a eulogy. Furthermore, the three tenors would be flying in from Europe to sing "Ave Maria."

I wondered if that ceremony, so full of pomp and circumstance, would be taking place before or after Edwina Carrington Fione had Charlie cremated. And I wondered if Father Fione had any notion that his brother's remains were scheduled for a final fling from the stern of an Ashes Away cruise, during which the grieving widow would be attempting to channel her late husband's spirit.

Mom dashed into my bedroom and, looking lovely in a taupe-and-sand wool cape, deposited yet another overdone bagel on the night table, saying as she whirled through the door, "Good-bye, darling, I'm off to church. Aaron will try to be here around seven. Gypsy Rose is bringing lasagna. Will you be back? Maybe we can play Scrabble? Give our minds a night off from murder. Now be a good ghost and confess all to Ben!"

She was gone before I could respond. That happened a lot. My mother really didn't want any answers. Monologues worked better for her. Just as well. I'd decided that after my brunch with Rickie Romero, I'd pay a visit to Sacred Heart Church to have my own interview with

Charlie Fione's brother. And that answer would have led my mother to a real inquisition!

. . . . .

It stopped raining as soon as I stepped under the small, crisp, red canopy. Bistro du Nord, a tiny, two-tiered restaurant, was located on the southwest corner of Ninety-third Street and Madison Avenue, directly across from the Corner Bookstore. Mom and I were steady patrons. The French fare was wonderful, the atmosphere was charming, and the prices were right, featuring a three-course pretheater dinner, including the best café au lait this side of Paris, for under twenty dollars.

Rickie Romero, dressed in a gray cashmere turtleneck, tweed jacket, and jeans, sat at a window table, engrossed in the same *New York Times* article that had grabbed my attention. As I approached, he folded the paper, stood up to greet me, took my hand in his, and gently pressed it against his lips. "*Bella* Jake. You bring the sunshine with you."

While Rickie ordered a Cosmopolitan for me and a Perrier for him, issuing instructions for prechilling the glasses and asking the waiter to drape my damp jacket over the back of my chair, I watched the people passing by. I loved Sundays on the Hill, the one day of the week when its residents took back their neighborhood. Mondays to Fridays, too many business types and intrepid shoppers filled the streets. Even the nannies, pushing prams, seemed to have a sense of purpose. And the private-school students, often, walked to and from their classes like Marines on dress parade. On Saturdays, visitors from the outer boroughs joined the tourists from Sioux City or Butte, who'd discovered that Carnegie Hill was only a short subway ride from Times Square, and ran amok from Central Park to Lexington. The museums and restaurants became cluttered with pastel-colored jogging suits, baseball caps featuring midwestern logos, and sneakers with soles as high as wedgies. But on Sundays, the home team reclaimed their turf.

Finished with his fussing, Rickie focused on me. "Are you comfortable? These tables are so small that they make my former prison cell look like the Gritti Palace."

"Ah, yes, Venice! One of my favorite chapters in your book. So romantic. Did you really steal the emeralds and sweep the princess off her feet?"

"Jake, *cara,* it's a novel." Rickie's long-enough-for-a-bird-to-nest left eyelash closed in a wink. "By definition, that would be fiction, wouldn't it?"

I laughed. This man was so damn handsome that he made me nervous. Then, of course, he could be a killer. As Holly's heir, he had the best motive of all. "But we writers know that first novels are always somewhat autobiographical, don't we?" It occurred to me that most of our conversation so far had consisted of questions. Not unlike being with my mother. "Don't worry, your secrets are safe with me." Feeling foolish, I lowered my own rather stubby lashes, hoping I wouldn't wind up with mascara in my eye sockets. I'd never been any good at flirting.

"No secrets." Rickie shrugged. "Thanks to the trial, my life's an open book. And I'd rather talk about you, Jake."

The waiter arrived with our drinks and I tried another tack. "You must feel like you have a new lease on life, missing death by a sip, so to speak."

"Actually, AA gave me a new lease on life. I committed most of my cat burglaries under the influence of alcohol. So the program saved my life twice, you see.

I'm really grateful." Rickie raised his glass of Perrier as if it were the finest champagne. "Think of all that I would have missed, like being here with you. *Salut!* I drink to your beauty, my freedom, and the sunshine!"

I took a long swallow from my Cosmopolitan. "Well, as one mystery writer to another, how many of the people on the panel do you think the killer wanted dead? One of you? Two of you? Or all three of you?"

"Thinking of doing a true-crime book, *cara?*" Rickie frowned. "I believe you heard me tell that old sot Maurice Welch this is my story to write. I've already signed a contract with my publisher. And the first chapter's finished and in the hands of the editor."

I was getting nowhere . . . fast. Romero sounded so smug. So proud of himself. So in control. So cold. Maybe he did do it! As Mom had pointed out, we were dealing with a cold-blooded killer. In addition to inheriting Holly's estate, Rickie might have orchestrated the St. Patrick's Day poisonings to get another book deal!

"Now"—Rickie smiled at me—"let's order. I suggest the salmon and shirred eggs over spinach."

As if Maura O'Hara's daughter would ever eat that! I ordered melon, scrambled eggs, and french fries. With ketchup. Then he launched into a long, rambling monologue about his ferry ride to the Statue of Liberty earlier this morning.

I tuned Rickie out, plotting how to turn this conversation back to *Cat on Trump Tower's Roof,* which we were supposedly here to discuss. What writer doesn't want to talk about his book? As the café au lait and crème caramel were being served, I decided to try again. And to be bold about it.

The Carita connection hadn't leapt off the pages. I

could understand why Mom might have missed it. As I'd read about the two frolicking friends and the cat burglar's visit, another pair of New Age writers had come to mind. But I still felt that it would be my best shot. "Carita Magenta claims—or complains—that your most intriguing chapter is really all about her and Venus DeMill. Any truth to that?"

Rickie dropped his fork and pointed his knife at me. "Did that poor deranged woman Wanda Sparks tell you that?"

"No," I said. His scowl startled me. "Carita herself told a friend of mine. These things tend to get around, you know." I hoped I sounded surer than I felt.

"Don't believe everything you hear, *bella*." His voice resumed its silky texture. "Magenta would sell her soul and Venus DeMill's as well, for a paragraph of publicity. Good or bad."

Though I didn't doubt his assessment of Carita's character, I figured Rickie had decided to rely on the nuts-and-sluts defense. "So, then that chapter wasn't based on Magenta and DeMill?"

"As I said in the beginning, it's fiction. Pure—or in those pages not so pure—fiction." I almost believed him. "Now, *bella* Jake, tell me about you. What sort of mysteries do you write?"

"Other people's. I'm a ghost."

The look that crossed his fine features could only be described as total disgust. My book-review brunch had come to an end.

Fourteen

Almost two o'clock and I still hadn't heard from Ben. I stopped at City Bank's ATM on Madison Avenue on my way down to Eighty-sixth Street to grab a crosstown bus and withdrew fifty dollars, dropping my balance to an all-time low. Then I pulled out my cell phone and punched number one, Ben's office. "Homicide," a familiar voice said.

"Aaron, is that you? This is Jake, I'm trying to track Ben down."

"So your mother said. He's making the rounds while I'm cutting through the paper chase. I know he had an appointment with the coroner and then planned on seeing Mrs. Fione after that." Aaron sighed. "The senator's widow wants to make his funeral arrangements and is demanding that the body be released."

"Did Ben get my message? It's really important that I speak to him."

"I don't know when he'll be back. Anything I can help you with?" Based on Aaron's evasive answer, I gathered that Ben had received my message but hadn't considered it to be high priority.

"Yes, you can tell Ben that . . ." What? What did I want Aaron to tell Ben? That Hunter couldn't be the killer because I'd come up with several other motives? Ben might be better informed than I was, regarding all of the suspects' motives, means, and opportunities. Anyway, I'd been thinking that Ben's first choice, Rickie Romero, could be the correct one. Since I kept changing my own opinion, what were my conclusions worth? "Never mind, Aaron, just tell him I called. Maybe Ben can stop by with you tonight. Even if it's only for a few minutes. Thanks." I hung up before he could ask me any more questions.

Boarding the bus, I asked for a transfer, shut off my phone, and took a seat behind a teenage boy, traveling with a portable entertainment center. Hard rock, blaring at a deafening decibel level, had accompanied me down the aisle. "Turn that down!" the driver yelled. Several passengers applauded. The kid surprised me and obeyed. As we drove past Central Park's old police station, I felt discouraged but determined, feeling that somehow, Hell's Kitchen held the answer.

I had a long wait for the downtown bus on Columbus Avenue. Sunday schedule, I assumed. The rain started again and my umbrella swayed in the wind. If a cab cruised by, I'd grab it, cost be damned. But every passing taxi that I hailed either held a passenger or sported an off-duty sign. Fifteen minutes later, wet and wind-blown, I boarded a crowded bus.

An excited group of chatty, well-dressed little old ladies, en route to a canasta tournament, exited at Seventy-eighth Street and I slipped into one of their seats. Rain pelted against its windows as the bus crawled through the traffic, picking up and depositing passengers at every stop. This would be one long ride. I closed my eyes and considered the case.

Of course, what I hadn't learned from Rickie Romero could fill a book. One evasive, annoyingly charming, and no doubt dangerous man. Naturally, he tweaked my interest. I'd planned to find out about his arrangements with Wanda, how he'd dealt with Hunter Green, and what connection he might have had with Hell's Kitchen. And, most importantly, his relationship with Holly Halligan. How, why, and when had he become her heir? Instead, cagey and taking total control, Rickie had danced away from any uncomfortable questions and had led me up the it's-all-only-fiction-isn't-it path.

Some other things had been nagging at me. For openers, a vignette in the Plaza lobby. Right after Carita Magenta had attacked Donald Jay, she'd engaged in a dialogue with Wanda Sparks, holding her back from her assigned task of retrieving Maurice Welch from his stool in the Oak Room bar. Since Wanda knew Donald Jay's attitude toward employees disobeying his commands, what had Carita told Wanda to stop her dead in her tracks?

Later, up in Gypsy Rose's suite, she'd mentioned that Ashley Butler had told her someone had ghosted Carita Magenta's color-me-comatose books. Could that be true? And if so, could that ghost be Wanda Sparks? I made a mental note to ask Gypsy Rose for more details about Ashley's and her chat at the Algonquin.

And had Maurice been less loaded than he'd appeared to be? He certainly sobered up fast after the panel had been poisoned. Did his purchase of an Ashes Away cruise mean that a lifetime of booze, red meat, and wild women had caught up with him? Was Welch ill? Or was he, as Holly Halligan had urged all prospective passengers to do, merely planning ahead? After all, he'd scheduled a date to marry Venus DeMill, hadn't he?

Finally, during the séance Holly Halligan had hinted of her own failed relationship with Maurice Welch. If that were true, when, where, and how had the romance started? And why wouldn't the press have picked up on it? Any affair, during any decade, between those two scene-stealing, internationally known egotists would have been tailor-made for the tabloids. Had Holly kept a diary or a log of her loves? I'd ask Dennis. Could the poisonings have been a crime of passion? Would Maurice have killed Holly because she'd broken his heart? I eliminated that as a possible motive. Whatever his faults, Maurice Welch wouldn't have killed two innocent people in order to avenge Holly Halligan's rejection. Would he?

I'd become so engrossed in death that Columbus had turned into Ninth Avenue and I'd missed my stop. Hopping off on Forty-eighth Street, I opened my umbrella and backtracked.

The cross atop the Church of the Sacred Heart graced an otherwise bleak neighborhood. Urban renewal hadn't hit Hell's Kitchen. At least not where I stood on the intersection of Ninth Avenue and Fifty-first Street. Old-timers, who'd lived there forever, referred to this area of Clinton as "one stop above Hell's Kitchen." Despite those purists' best efforts, the West Side, from about Thirty-ninth to Fifty-ninth, retained its better-known, hotter-than-hell nickname. In a way, I'd returned to my roots. Working-class Irish once had been Sacred Heart's largest group of parishioners. My maternal grandfather had grown up two blocks away from here and had attended Sacred Heart grammar school, around the corner on Fifty-second Street, graduating in 1920. I'd just walked past his old tenement that Mom, as a committee of one, considered a landmark building and other historians considered a slum, on my way from the bus stop.

Today, few Irish families remained; the primary population of the parish and its school consisted of more recent arrivals, including those from Puerto Rico, Central America, the Philippines, and Asia.

I walked in on a wedding. The church's curved pews were decorated with white and red roses and filled with happy people wearing colorful clothing and big smiles. The ceremony was in Spanish and the bride, a stunning, slim beauty, dressed in yards of lace, with a matching mantilla draped over a crown of black braids, sauntered down the aisle as elegantly as a haute couture runway model.

A large, rather stark canopy framed the altar, contrasting sharply with the aged, dark wood on the confessional booths' closed doors, just as the modern stained-glass windows seemed incongruous with the curved wooden arches of the old choir loft in the back of the church. The interior had been redone in the sixties and much of Sacred Heart's nineteenth-century charm and sanctity had been replaced with what one longtime parishioner had described to Mom as a less holy, more mod look.

The bride and groom held hands, lovingly gazed into each other's eyes, and recited their vows in front of a young Hispanic priest. Father Fione was nowhere in sight. I decided to try the rectory.

Suspecting Father Fione wouldn't be averse to more publicity, I introduced myself as a writer, and an elderly housekeeper ushered me into a dark foyer, furnished only with a bench, an ancient, wooden umbrella stand/coatrack, a drooping potted plant, and a large crucifix.

"Father's in the den. I'll tell him you're here."

A comfortable olive corduroy couch was separated from two olive-and-white-print club chairs by a round oak coffee table. The pastor stood behind an old oak desk, covered with haphazard piles of paper.

Joseph Fione, taller and slimmer than his brother but with the same thatch of thick gray hair and dark brown eyes, crossed the room to greet me and gave me a tight smile as he shook my hand. "Please have a seat, Miss O'Hara." No Ms. for this man.

"I'm so sorry about Senator Fione and I won't take up much of your time, Father." I almost started a schoolgirl curtsy that I'd learned long ago at another, very different, Sacred Heart school up in Carnegie Hill. "You must be very busy with the funeral plans."

"No, no, my dear, the Mass has been set for Tuesday at ten A.M. And Mrs. Fione is handling the burial arrangements. Now, what would you like to know?" My deference seemed to have paid off.

I sat in one of the club chairs, keeping my feet close together and flat on the floor, continuing the convent-schoolgirl image. "Your quotes in today's *Times* were most intriguing. I'd like to hear more about your childhood. And the senator's, too."

"What paper are you with, Miss O'Hara?" He'd been sitting, relaxed, in the other chair. Now both his voice and his body language stiffened.

"I'm an author, Father Fione. This is research, background for a book." I wasn't exactly lying to a priest; I might need the information I hoped to get, someday, somehow, in some future project.

"A biography of Charlie?" his brother asked.

"Well, er, more of a nonfiction novel, if you would.

Er—in the style of *In Cold Blood*." I cringed at my boldness and at how easily I misled.

Father Fione nodded. "That's an ambitious undertaking, isn't it, Miss O'Hara?"

"Dennis Kim suggested it." A total lie. Dennis would kill me and I'd probably go straight to hell! And never get to see Zelda Fitzgerald, Emily Brontë, or Jack O'Hara. But that didn't stop me. "He's representing the cardinal with his new book, you know."

Warmth flooded Father Joseph Fione's smile, "Ask away, Miss O'Hara."

"I do realize that discussing the senator's death is painful for you, but I'd like to know if either Holly Halligan or Rickie Romero had ever been part of his life. Doesn't it strike you odd that someone tried to kill all three of them? There must have been a connection!"

"A detective from homicide is stopping by in an hour or so; I'll bet he asks those same questions. And my answer will be the same." The priest shook his head from side to side. "Not as far as I know."

"What about when you were kids, here in Hell's Kitchen? No family named Romero? No Halligans?"

"None that I can recall. And my brother has never mentioned either Miss Halligan or Mr. Romero to me. Neither long ago, nor recently."

Modesty's news bulletin from our postmortem at the Plaza suite flashed through my mind. Some of the senator's last words had been addressed to Holly Halligan. Only he hadn't used that name. "How about Houlihan, Father? Did you grow up with anyone called Houlihan?"

All his cheek color as well as his smile faded. "Why, yes. The Houlihan family lived in our building. But how could you know that?"

I spoke gently. "I'm sure the police will be asking

you the same thing. The senator definitely had met Holly
Halligan prior to their panel appearance, and on the day
of his death, he referred to her as Helen Mary Houlihan."

Father Fione stood. "The Houlihans only had boys.
Three sons. All older than Charlie, Fatima, and me.
Now, I'm sorry, Miss O'Hara, but there's nothing more
to dicuss. I'd prefer to address this matter with the
proper authorities." I'd been dismissed.

The weather had cleared up. In front of the church,
the bride and groom were posing for pictures in bright
sunshine. I walked south on Ninth Avenue, stopping at
a bodega to buy a Cuban coffee, and sipped it at a sidewalk table. Even Hell's Kitchen had discovered the joys
of al fresco dining—though the street smells were less
than delightful. I called Modesty.

"Jake, I'm in the middle of a chapter!" With her
gothic novel at 2,600 pages, did I expect her to be anywhere else? "What do you want?"

"Look, I need a favor, fast. I'm one step ahead of Ben
Rubin and I want to stay there." I appealed to Modesty's
baser emotions. I knew she'd want to be party to any
scheme that outsmarted the police. "Can you bring up
the obit and any articles on Charlie Fione. I'm sitting in
Hell's Kitchen. I need the address where he grew up."

"Give me a minute to save my stuff and I'll pull up
today's *Times*."

I took another sip of my coffee. Excellent. And
watched the strollers. Then Modesty was back. "Listen,
Jake, Too Tall Tom's over at Maurice Welch's apartment as we speak. When he finishes there, he wants to
get together tonight, okay?"

"Yeah, I'll call when I get home. Let's try to meet
around seven. Mom's planning a Scrabble game with
Aaron and Gypsy Rose. Ben may be stopping by, but

I'm sure that will be a brief encounter . . . if it even happens."

"Right." I could actually hear the buzzing from Modesty's computer. "Now here's what you wanted. Fione's obit says that the senator spent his childhood in a tenement on Forty-ninth Street between Ninth and Tenth. No address. I guess you could knock on doors. Say you're the Avon lady."

I finished my coffee and touched up my makeup.

Four doors east of Tenth Avenue, after striking out a dozen times, I found my source. An old lady, dressed in purple, sat in a red, canvas beach chair on the stoop of a brownstone, her face turned toward the late-afternoon sun. Though both the house and the lady had seen better days, the latter had bright eyes, good posture, and an air of anticipation. Which, since she had to be ninety, seemed remarkable.

"Hi!" I said, smiling. "I'm Jake O'Hara, a writer. And I'm wondering if Senator Fione might have grown up in this house."

"He did," she said in a firm voice. "And a bold one he was, wasn't he?"

I nodded. "His brother, too? I mean, was he bold as well?"

"How many times did I tell Mr. Casey that Joey would wind up a priest. Forever twirling them rosary beads! The boy was enough to drive a body away from any devotion at all to the Blessed Virgin Mother."

"Is Mr. Casey your husband?"

"Was. Dead and gone these last fifty-five years."

"Sorry." I said, thinking I sounded inane. The man had been dead for over a half century. "Tell me about the Fione family. Did you know them well?"

"Having no children of my own, I used to baby-sit

for Maria Fione. Charlie could be a real handful, but Joey and Fatima—her mother named her for the miracle—were good kids." Mrs. Casey grinned at me. Her teeth looked real. "Except, between you and me, dearie, Joey was a religious fanatic. Always dressing up like a nun, you know."

"Mrs. Casey, did you know the Houlihans?"

"I called them the hooligans! And I was right, wasn't I? Two of them boys are dead of the drink. The third brother wound up in jail."

"They had no sisters? No one in the family was called Helen Mary Houlihan? This is really important, Mrs. Casey."

"No, didn't I just tell you, there were three sons." She pulled her heavy, purple wool cardigan tighter across her chest. "It's getting too cold, I'm going upstairs." As she struggled to close the beach chair, I reached over and did it for her. "Wait a minute! I think Helen Mary might be the name of the girl who visited that dreadful summer."

"What summer would we be talking about, Mrs. Casey?"

"That hot one, fifty-five years ago, the summer my husband died of cancer. A cousin came to stay with the Houlihans for the month of August. Terrible warm, it was. The worst August I ever remember. Anyway, my Michael finally died on the feast of the Assumption. The heat was hell and that young woman was even hotter. Trouble incarnate. Wearing tight white shorts and a halter top. Teasing the fellows. And she should have known better; she was older than all the boys, had to be in her early twenties. I'm pretty sure her name was Helen Mary. Something bad happened and she left town, sudden like, and returned home. Upstate, I think."

God! "What happened?"

"I never did find out. All I know is that was the summer the oldest Houlihan boy threatened to kill Charlie Fione."

Fifteen

The sky had grown dark by the time I'd finished canvassing the rest of the block. Not surprisingly, none of the other residents could recall that eventful summer from fifty-five years ago. On the whole, the people of Hell's Kitchen had impressed me. Though I'd run into a few gang members, dressed in black leather and strutting menacingly up and down the avenue, mostly I'd spoken to lots of polite kids, even if their English was limited. While their parents and grandparents had remained somewhat wary, no one had ordered me off the premises.

Since I'd decided to call it a day, Ben had weighed heavily on my mind. I wanted to see him. To talk about this frustrating case's twists and turns. To give him a hug. Maybe he'd be there when I arrived home. And I felt edgy. For the last few minutes I'd sensed that someone was watching me. Nervous, I looked over my shoulder. No one. And everyone. The just-lighted street lamps cast deep shadows, and as evening approached, suddenly all of Hell Kitchen's denizens seemed dangerous.

Picking up speed, I glanced back again. A big man with broad shoulders had appeared on the scene, almost on my heels. My heart felt tight, bile flooded my throat, and despite the cool air, sweat trickled down from my hair.

I felt two firm hands grab me. Kicking frantically, I tried to swing around. But I was shoved to the ground and a huge body lay on top of me. No sound came out when I tried to yell. A loud clatter directly in front of me caused my eyes to fly open. A large bucket of blood had landed inches from my nose; as it rolled toward the gutter, its contents splattered everywhere. Red liquid stained my free hand. I could smell it. What the hell? Not blood. Paint! I tried to raise my head, but the man had me pinned to the ground. There were noises above me; a crowd had gathered. The sounds made no sense. Then I heard an ungodly shriek and realized that I'd been the one who'd screamed.

A soft voice whispered in my ear, "Sorry I scared you, lady, but that bucket was aimed right for your head!" As he spoke, he rolled off my back and helped me to my feet.

Dazed, I stared up into concerned, dark eyes. My Hell's Kitchen angel. A middle-aged guy in faded Levi's and a Yankee jacket. "Thank you." I didn't recognize my own voice. "God, thank you."

Most of the crowd had moved on, but several people hovered, recapping the bucket's descent and asking how I felt. Still wobbly, I tried to smile. One attractive young woman said, "I saw the whole thing. Someone reached out from that rooftop"—she pointed to the five-story building directly behind us—"and deliberately dropped that old pail down. Aimed it straight at your head."

"A man or a woman?" I croaked. It finally had dawned on me that we were in front of Mrs. Casey's brownstone. The house where the Houlihans and the Fiones had lived so long ago.

"Couldn't tell you," the young woman was saying, "but the person's outstretched arms were covered in a dark color. Black, I think, and probably a sweater."

The big man picked up the wooden bucket and examined it. "I guess someone really wanted to send you a message, lady." He pointed to crude printing, the large letters covering half of one side of the bucket and written with the same red paint that now stained the sidewalk and most of my right hand: BUTT OUT! As if my butt would fit in that bucket. My protector sniffed the inside of the pail. "Turpentine was used to thin that paint. Could have caused a lot of damage if it had landed in your eyes."

A patrol car pulled up. A young cop rolled down the window. "Trouble?"

All eyes were on me. "No, Officer," I said. "Someone seems to have spilled a bucket of paint. An accident. But everything is all right. Thank you anyway."

The cop stared at me. "Yeah. Sure. Well, then that *someone* should clean up his colorful *accident*." He drove off.

I extended my hand to the man who'd tackled me. "I'm Jake O'Hara."

"James Roosevelt." He grinned. "I like a woman who wouldn't tell a cop if the sun was shining." The crowd echoed his approval. "And don't worry, Jake O'Hara, I live right in this building, I'll get some paint remover from my place and see what I can do about that bloody mess."

"Again, I thank you and I'd like to ask you a question.

How could a nonresident get onto the roof of your building? Isn't the door kept locked?"

"Yeah, it's locked, but from the outside. We're trying to keep the bad guys out, not the tenants in."

"If a resident went out on the roof, he'd have to use a key to get back inside. Is that correct?"

"Yes. It's the same key that opens the front door."

"And, if an outsider went out on the roof, he'd have to keep the door propped open in order to get back into the stairwell, right?"

"Right."

"How could a stranger get into the building? I mean if he had no key."

"Well, the guy could have a reason for being in the building. Like a repairman or a meter reader. But never on a Sunday. Or he could ring one of the apartments and a tenant could buzz him in, I guess."

"But a tenant wouldn't let someone that he didn't know in, would he?"

James Roosevelt laughed. "A few of those old folks don't remember who they know. So that's a possibility. Hey, you've asked a lot more than one question and you're looking pretty beat. Let's put you in a taxi."

Stepping into the cab, I said, "I'll be in touch, Mr. Roosevelt."

"My friends call me Jimmy." He patted my sore right shoulder. "And I'll look forward to that visit, Jake."

Sixteen

I'd hoped to slink into the house and get cleaned up without anyone seeing me. The grit and grime of Hell's Kitchen clung to my clothes and I smelled as if I'd been rolling around on a centuries-old, filthy sidewalk. Which, in fact, I had.

But no sneaking through the co-op for me. Mom had a gaggle of guests and they all swooped down on me as soon as I walked in the door.

"Where have you been all day?" my mother led off, sounding as indignant as if she'd advised me of her whereabouts at all times.

Too Tall Tom sniffed. "Interesting aroma. What in the world have you been up to this afternoon, darling? After spending the better part of my afternoon with Maurice Welch, I'm sure he's our killer." Too Tall Tom, once again, had rushed to judgment . . . convinced that the first suspect he interviewed would turn out to be the guilty one.

"I really need to talk to you, Jake!" Modesty grabbed

my arm. "When you never called me back, we decided to meet here. Wanda's studio has been ransacked. And some important evidence is missing!"

Aaron looked worried. "Ben's on his way. He said to tell you he was sorry he didn't get back to you, but he finally has some time to listen to your theories. He also hoped that you weren't out playing detective. No such luck, huh?" He shook his head and went down the four wide wooden steps into the living room and reached for one of the small bamboo-and-cane chairs on either side of the staircase, bringing it up to the foyer. "Sit down, Jake, you look exhausted."

Jane's brown eyes darted from the garish red stain on my hand to my dirty, rumpled parka. "Good God, you weren't attacked or raped, were you?"

My mother groaned. Then collapsed onto the bamboo chair.

Gypsy Rose, wearing a lace apron over a brown silk Chanel suit and holding a strainer in one hand and a box of egg noodles in the other, said, "Jake, dear, why don't you grab a nice, hot shower? The pot roast will be ready in fifteen minutes. We can discuss everything over dinner."

I gave her a grateful smile. "That sounds like a plan." I fled into my room and locked the door behind me.

My message light was flashing; both Hunter Green and Ashley Butler had called. As curious as I felt about what they wanted to tell me, I'd have to put them on hold. For now, my plate was full.

Not wanting to leave my room to scour the kitchen cabinets for turpentine, I tried to remove the red paint with nail-polish remover. Other than adding yet another unpleasant odor to my totally smelly person, it didn't do a damn thing. I'd just have to live awhile longer with my battle scars.

Piling my clothes in a corner, I stepped into the shower, soaped up, and scrubbed. Letting the warm water hammer my aching body, soaking then shampooing my hair, and trying not to think, I began to feel somewhat better. Then I lathered Vaseline Intensive Care lotion from face to feet—*Jesus, I was turning into my mother*—towel-dried my hair, and dressed in a well-worn, faded, soft jogging suit and old, white socks. If I didn't take away everyone's appetite, I was ready to join our guests for dinner.

They'd gathered 'round the table. The three ghosts grouped together at one end, in front of the bay window, with Modesty in the middle. Aaron sat to Jane's right, slicing the beef; Mom was on Too Tall Tom's left, and Ben stood behind the chair next to Mom's, gesturing for me to sit down beside him. Gypsy Rose, who was pouring red wine from Nana's Waterford decanter, would be seated between Aaron and me. With eight of us to feed, including the bottomless pit that was Too Tall Tom, I hoped she'd cooked a lot of food.

As Ben planted a perfunctory peck on my greasy cheek, I reached for my wine goblet. "So, how are you doing?" he asked, using his finest NYPD homicide detective voice. I drained my glass; this could be a difficult dinner.

"Fine," I said, placing my red-stained hand on Ben's forearm, patting it quickly, and then turning my complete attention to Modesty. Knowing that she could talk straight through the main course. Counting on it. "Tell me about what happened to Wanda Sparks. When did you speak to her?"

"Right after you called me from Hell's Kitchen,"

Modesty began, eliciting a dirty look from my mother and a snide chuckle from Ben. Naturally, Modesty ignored them both. She held center stage and wouldn't abridge a line to spare anyone. Including me. "Wanda was hysterical. Said she'd come home from work—"

"On a Sunday?" I asked.

"Yes. Donald Jay had insisted that she meet him at the Plaza. Claimed there was urgent paperwork that had to be taken care of immediately. But then, get this, when Wanda arrived at the hotel, he wasn't in his room. She had him paged, but no one could locate him. Anyway, while she'd been trucking up to Fifty-ninth Street and searching for Donald, someone had trashed her apartment."

"And removed evidence!" my mother said.

"That poor, unfortunate young woman," Gypsy Rose said. "None of her lives has been easy. And Donald Jay continues to be part of Wanda's unfinished destiny." I wondered if she'd had a psychic experience while peeling the carrots that I now passed to Ben.

"What evidence would that be?" Aaron asked.

Modesty gave me a sheepish glance, then blurted, "Some papers that reveal, among other things, a strong connection between Holly Halligan and Rickie Romero. They also contained proof positive, according to Wanda, that she—not Rickie—wrote most of *Cat on Trump Tower's Roof*!" So much for Modesty's keeping secrets from the police or, apparently, from anyone in listening range of her big mouth. Since I'd started the questioning, I should have been prepared for any answer. Still I couldn't believe that Modesty, who'd been acting as Wanda's temporary sponsor, had broken her anonymity.

"Is someone on top of this?" Aaron asked Ben.

"Yes, Dad. Ms. Sparks reported the breaking and entering to 911 as well as to Modesty. Cassidy's at her apartment now, taking a statement."

I felt better. Wanda had given the police all this information herself. Modesty wasn't breaking one of our Ghostwriters Anonymous traditions. If she had been, Jane would have kicked her from here to eternity. Obviously, Too Tall Tom and Jane had heard the whole story. And understood that Wanda had spilled her own secrets. Now I felt guilty about doubting Modesty. I smiled at her and asked, "Well, why did Holly Halligan leave the bulk of her estate to Rickie?"

Modesty served herself a huge portion of noodles; I knew she wouldn't touch the pot roast. Good, Too Tall Tom was devouring his. "Wanda wasn't too coherent, but I think she said that Holly had once been in love with Rickie Romero's father. A very long time ago. Or maybe it was his grandfather."

Could that love affair have taken place in Hell's Kitchen, during a long, hot August, fifty-five years ago? I wondered.

"Where?" I asked Modesty.

"I don't know where." Modesty added butter to her noodles. "Why is where important? Let's see, I believe Wanda told me Rickie Romero originally came from upstate New York. Plattsburgh, I think." As she spoke, it sank in. For both of us. "God!" Modesty dropped her knife. "That's the same town where Wanda said the waste-management site—that Senator Fione would be voting against—is located!"

"And the town where Donald Jay's motive for murder can be found!" Jane said.

I suspected that Plattsburgh might harbor yet another motive for murder.

"Just how do you know about Plattsburgh, Jane?" Modesty asked.

"Ashley Butler told me. This very afternoon. I ran into her and Dennis Kim." My toe twitched in my sticky sock. "I'd gone out for a late lunch with my editor. The galleys needed so much rewriting! I really blame the copy editor. No one has a command of grammar anymore." I could hear Modesty snicker.

But Jane, blissfully, rattled on. "They were at Sarabeth's, having tea." How dare Dennis take that woman and her totally tacky hair to tea in my favorite place? "And Ashley was complaining about working for a possible killer. Says she's scared to death of her boss. She insists that Donald Jay had more than a million reasons for wanting Charlie Fione dead. And it had to be fast! Before the Senate's final vote on that environmental bill this coming week."

Modesty, not about to be upstaged by Jane, jumped in and explained, in depth, to the rest of her audience what Wanda had told us the night before regarding the Plattsburgh waste-management site's being a motive for murder.

Ben kept a poker face, but I'd bet the Wedgwood that he'd already heard this story from Donald Jay.

Gypsy Rose asked Aaron to pass the platter back to Too Tall Tom. I shoved my noodles into my carrots and pushed the pot roast around in circles. On information overload, I'd lost my appetite. My stomach gurgled, my muscles felt tense, my head ached, and Too Tall Tom hadn't told his tale yet.

My mother missed nothing. "You're not eating, Jake." I speared a noodle. Ben, who seemed to be off in his own world—probably Plattsburgh—hadn't eaten much either. But I didn't hear his father commenting on his less-than-clean plate.

I turned to Jane, figuring Modesty had savored her shining moment, but all great performances require a finale. "Did Ashley have anything else to say?" What I ached to know was why Ashley and Dennis had been together. A business meeting? On a Sunday? Maybe. He had arranged a business dinner with her on Friday night, before accepting Gypsy Rose's invitation to the Tavern on the Green. Dennis couldn't be romantically involved with Ashley, could he? I flexed my feet, seriously resenting Dennis Kim for causing so much turmoil in my toes.

Jane said, "Actually, Ashley did mention that earlier today she'd witnessed—her word choice, not mine—you and Rickie Romero enjoying a cozy brunch and each other's company at Bistro du Nord."

Ben snapped out of his reverie and said, "Jake, you've had a busy day and we still haven't discovered how you acquired those bloodred streaks."

I gave Jane a fierce frown, which, as intended, flustered her. "Well, er, I told Ashley," she said, "that you had some questions regarding Rickie's book . . . I mean . . . well, we know you weren't on a date . . ." Jane shut up, obviously, having no finish.

Great! Damned if I did have a rendezvous with Rickie and damned if I didn't. Should I just come clean, forgetting about a cover story and admitting to my Nancy Drew ploy? A rather unsuccessful one at that. What the hell? I was a citizen of a free country. As a mystery writer who'd witnessed a double murder, I had every right to question a suspect. Regardless of what Ben, Mom, or Zelda Fitzgerald had to say. Playing detective might be dangerous, but it was no crime. I sat up straight and gave a synopsis of my book-review brunch.

Too Tall Tom had managed to put away two helpings of everything while the rest of us were listening to Modesty and asking questions. When I closed the chapter on Rickie's and my conversation, I turned to him. "Okay, why do you believe Maurice Welch is our killer?"

"Motive, motive, motive. The old boy up is to his enlarged liver in them!" Too Tall Tom sighed. "Why is it I always get stuck with the drunks? He insisted that I have a second Manhattan, and as I was about to leave, he was mixing his fifth. By then he'd run out of sweet vermouth, but had become extremely loose in the lips. Positively, a blabbing brook, simply spewing out his hatred for Holly Halligan. And he had reasons for wanting Rickie Romero dead as well."

"Like what?" Gypsy Rose asked.

"Let's start with Holly," Too Tall Tom said. "Welch is an old souse, that's why he looks like death warmed over; however, he says he's never felt better. And he's determined to marry the Venus Flytrap. The wedding's scheduled for next weekend—at the Waldorf. Grand Ballroom. As you all know, Maurice booked a cremation cruise with Holly—says he believes in planning ahead—and because of their long-ago affair, she promised to give him a discount. He even asked her to be his designated flinger. Since they'd once been lovers, Maurice claims he didn't bother reading the fine print in the contract and that now he owes Ashes Away almost five hundred thousand dollars. Welch says he's nowhere near ready to take that cruise, but the company's dunning him. Holly's arrangements for her former boyfriend's final voyage included a sixty-foot yacht berthed off the coast of New Zealand, the purchase of a solid gold urn, and booking Reverend Sharpton to deliver the eulogy.

Of course, as Holly's heir, most of that half million would wind up in Rickie Romero's hands."

"Wait a minute!" my mother said. "When and where did this affair between Holly and Maurice take place? And did it end amicably?"

Too Tall Tom grinned. "In Hollywood, Maura, during the mid-fifties. Welch was out on the coast, writing one of Holly's ski epics, but it was the affair that went downhill. She left him for Errol Flynn."

"I can certainly understand that." Gypsy Rose cleared away Ben's plate, adding it to a stack she'd amassed. "Zelda has told me Holly's ensconced on the same plane with Errol. This bit of gossip explains that, doesn't it?" She left the dining room without waiting for an answer.

"Maurice hasn't booked a appointment with Dr. Assisted Suicide, has he?" I asked.

Ben threw his napkin on the table. "Jake, I gather that Dennis the Menace, in addition to divulging the contents of Holly Halligan's will, told you about Dr. Nujurian and you then informed the other ghosts."

Paying no attention to Ben's nasty tone, Too Tall Tom moved on. "No. Maurice insists that though he's an old man, he loves life and Venus, and has no desire for an early departure."

"As such a lover of life, could he kill?" my mother asked.

"I'm certain he poisoned Holly! In addition to the inflated cost of the cruise, I don't believe he ever got over being dumped by her. And while admitting nothing, Welch confessed that after reading *Cat on Trump Tower's Roof*, he only hoped he'd live long enough to piss manhattans on Rickie Romero's grave!"

Gypsy Rose returned to the dining room and served us devil's-food cake and vanilla ice cream for dessert.

Seventeen

Ben hadn't kissed me good-bye. He'd passed on dessert as well, explaining that he had to get back on the job; however, at Gypsy Rose's cajoling, he accepted a quick cup of coffee. Then I told the group about my own adventurous afternoon, deleting only my suspicions about the bucket, making its descent sound more like mischief than malice. My mother reacted as if I'd been in imminent danger of death. Modesty had a second slice of cake.

With Ben's departure, we split into two factions. Mom, Gypsy Rose, and Aaron were sent to the living room to play Scrabble while the ghosts volunteered to do the dishes. I knew Mom hated turning her kitchen's cleanup over to anyone less anal-retentive than she, but Too Tall Tom and Jane actually might be even *cleaner.* I whispered that seven-letter word in Mom's ear, ushered her out through the white French doors, pulled the board game down from the shelf in the hall closet, and returned to find the kitchen had become an autoclave.

Once Jane had stacked all the dirty dishes in the nea-
test piles I'd ever seen and Too Tall Tom had searched
for and found new sponges, SOS pads, and a rubber
scraper to properly scrub the pots and pans, we settled
down to discuss in depth the complexities of this case
and its amazing cast of suspects.

No matter which way our sleuthing skewed, Too Tall
Tom continued to spout theories about how Maurice
Welch had done the deed. When I asked the ghosts if
any of them could hazard a guess as to why Carita Magenta had stopped Wanda in the Plaza lobby just before
she went to rescue Maurice from the Oak Room, Too
Tall Tom said, "Well, it's so clear, isn't it? Wanda's the
associate culprit. The poor thing may not have known
that she was an accomplice. Carita, acting as Maurice's
agent, probably only told her that Maurice wanted to
play a prank that required Wanda to dress up as a leprechaun and deliver a pitcher to the panel. Wanda
wouldn't have had any idea that the green beer had been
laced with cyanide. And Maurice hadn't known Rickie
was AA. Such a scary thought would never cross that
old drunk's mind. Then, afterward, Wanda must have
been terrified. And wouldn't—couldn't—tell the police.
Sad."

God! That theory actually made some sense. With
Carita knowing that Wanda had served the poison,
Wanda could never reveal that she'd been Carita's ghost.
If, in fact, she had. When we were finished in the
kitchen, I'd ask Gypsy Rose about that. Then, too,
Welch had suddenly sobered up after the poisonings.
Flying straight enough to try to interview Rickie . . .
wanting to turn the tragedy into a book! "But why would
Maurice have murdered the senator?" I asked. "He didn't
have anything against him, did he?"

"No motive that we're aware of at this point!" Jane attacked Nana's old cast-iron pot as if it carried the ebola virus. "That doesn't mean Maurice didn't have one. What if his and the senator's path, like his and Holly's, had crossed before? And we now know Maurice had wanted Rickie dead. Too Tall Tom could be on the right track."

Modesty cut herself another slice of devil's-food cake. "Have you all forgotten about Edwina Carrington? She booked an appointment for the senator to meet with Dr. Nujurian. Maybe he'd vetoed that and Edwina decided to speed up her husband's date with death. Charlie Fione had an ancient-history, secret connection of some sort with Holly Halligan, a.k.a. Helen Mary Houlihan, and Edwinda had good reason to want her out of the picture, too."

"Don't keep dirtying dishes, Modesty!" Too Tall Tom said. "We're washing the Wedgwood by hand. You're supposed to be drying!" He grabbed her plate. "If you're correct, why would the widow Carrington have wanted to kill Rickie Romero?"

"She didn't *want* him dead, silly," Modesty snarled. "She considered Rickie to be expendable, like one of those minks that was slaughtered to make her coat. His death simply served her purpose. Nothing personal, you understand."

Another murder motive I could live with. God, had I become jaded or what? I climbed up on the stepladder to put the china away in the corner cabinet.

"Well, after my brunch with the reticent Rickie, I think Ben's primary suspect could be our killer. Remember, he chatted with Wanda right before the panel started. She could have aided and abetted him. Inheriting all that money and the lucrative Ashes Away company gave Romero a major motive for killing Holly. Though I haven't a clue as to why Holly made him her heir, I do believe that Rickie, Holly, Hell's Kitchen, and Fione's past are, somehow, connected. And Wanda knows more than she's saying." I took another pile of plates from Jane.

"That's a stretch!" Modesty said. I knew she wasn't talking about my struggle to reach the top shelf. "Wanda Sparks might have been acting as a lone leprechaun. A frustrated ghost, full of resentment and without a program, could be capable of killing."

"I can reach up there without a ladder!" Too Tall Tom had turned away from arranging the glassware on a silver tray. The Waterford sparkled. Mom would be thrilled. "Come down this minute, Jake!" I obeyed at once. My shoulder still hurt. As he took my hand, he said, "Yes, Wanda had both the motive and the opportunity to rid herself of Rickie, but would she have poisoned the senator and Holly along with him?"

Jane switched on the dishwasher. Since she and Too Tall Tom seemed to have done everything by hand, I wondered what was in there. Then, wiping off the counter, she said, "I guess Magenta and DeMill would be wild cards. Though I must say a bucket of bright red paint being dropped on Jake's head smacks of color-me-comatose Carita. But how about Ashley Butler? She certainly could be the leprechaun. Someone's accomplice? Or did she have a motive of her own? She really tried to lay the blame on Donald Jay this afternoon. He only agreed to meet with me tomorrow morning after I told him I was a freelance writer for a crime magazine and we wanted to profile him. Fat chance. Both Wanda and Ashley think the Plattsburgh property could be his motive. With a man as sleazy as he's reputed to be, if I do a little digging, there may be more dirty deals."

I nodded. "Good! Try to find out if Donald Jay knew the Romero family in Plattsburgh. And Ashley is on my list. Ironically, I had messages from both her and Hunter when I arrived home this evening, but I haven't had a chance to call either of them back."

Jane dried her hands and smoothed out the dish towel. Then she hung it up; totally amazing—the linen towel looked as if it had just been ironed. "We all have to accept the obvious. Like it or not, Hunter Green has the best motive. Two, in fact. Revenge and greed. He hated Holly because of what she'd done to Angela and he knew where Rickie had stashed the Faith diamond."

"I'll never accept that Hunter's a killer!" I said.

"And neither will I!" Modesty, seconding my endorsement, surprised and pleased me.

When the ghosts had gone and Mom, Gypsy Rose, and Aaron started their Scrabble rematch—Gypsy Rose made two seven-letter words, winning the first game— I headed for my bedroom. All I wanted to do was crawl into bed, pull the comforter up to my chin, and sleep till Thursday, but I decided that I'd better return my calls first.

Hunter Green picked up on the first ring. "Jake, thank God!" He must have caller ID. "I've been pacing the loft, waiting to hear from you." God, I felt guilty about not talking to him sooner; I should have called this morning. Hunter must be terrified, thinking he'd be arrested any moment. And there was no excuse for not responding to his message before dinner.

"Sorry, Hunter. I've had a busy day, but you've been on my mind. And I've been trying to find out whodunit. Not that I've had much luck. Anyway, I'm here now. How can I help?"

"I really don't want to bother you, Jake, but I have no one else to turn to . . ." He sounded desperate.

"Please, Hunter, tell me what's wrong."

"Dr. Nujurian called late this afternoon. She received two threatening letters in the mail . . . and she accused me of sending them."

"When did the letters arrive?"

"One in Friday's mail and one yesterday. Dr. Nujurian is convinced that I poisoned Holly Halligan and is afraid I plan on murdering her, too. I denied sending them, but the only reason that she hasn't gone running to the police is because she 'doesn't want to deal with those fascists.' But, if another letter arrives tomorrow, she'll give them all to Ben Rubin. She must have gotten his name from the newspaper. If Dr. Nujurian does that, I'll be indicted for sure."

"And we have no way of knowing if there will be another letter tomorrow."

"Exactly! What am I going to do, Jake?"

"Listen to me, Hunter." My mouth ran faster than my mind, but I'd think of something. "Do nothing. Keep a low profile; stay at home. I'll handle this. Now promise me."

I dialed Modesty. "Is the ghostmobile fixed?" Her old Beetle had transported many of us ghosts when we left Manhattan for the outer boroughs, Long Island, or New Jersey.

"I'm picking it up at the garage in the morning. Why?" Modesty sounded suspicious.

"Hunter needs us. Will you drive me up to Westchester? We need to pay a visit to Dr. Nujurian."

"WHAT!"

Ten minutes later she agreed to my half-baked plan. While I was still mulling over a possible solution to

Hunter's problem, the phone rang. "Jake, this is Ashley." As if I wouldn't recognize those honeyed tones. "Dennis suggested that I talk to you. I need some advice. Can we meet sometime tomorrow?"

"Well, er, couldn't we discuss it on the phone?" Dennis Kim had to know that the last woman in the world I'd want to advise would be this Barbie doll.

Ashley actually gasped. "This is a matter of utmost secrecy and, of course, we can't discuss it on the phone."

I wanted to kill Dennis. Instead, I made a date with her for cocktails at six, tomorrow evening, in the Algonquin lobby. I hoped for Ashley's secret's sake that the CIA didn't hang out there. That reminded me of something else. I hopped out of bed, scurried to the living room, and interrupted the Scrabble game. "Gypsy Rose, when Ashley Butler suggested that someone else had written Carita's books, did she also suggest Wanda Sparks could be that ghost?"

"No." Gypsy Rose looked up, holding a tile in her hand. "Not that night at the Algonquin right before the Crime Writers' Conference, but on Friday night at Tavern on the Green, something Ashley said gave me the impression that she herself might be Carita's ghost. I forgot to tell you; so much has happened since then!"

"Thanks. Good night, gang." As I was leaving, Gypsy Rose made another seven-letter word: *ensnare*.

Eighteen

My mother sat in the breakfast nook reading the *Times* and sipping tea. A place had been set for me and there were bagels, a tub of cream cheese, and a pitcher of orange juice on the table. The sun streamed in through the windows, highlighting Mom in a hazy halo. She wore a beige jogging suit, my Yankee hat, and sneakers. I wore a chenille robe I've had since college and socks that served as slippers. "Good morning, Jake. I picked up fresh bagels, hot from the baker's oven, so they won't need to be toasted." Thank God! "Have one; the cinnamon-raisin ones are luscious and I'll pour you a nice cup of tea. You had a rough time yesterday, didn't you, dear?"

"You could say that, I guess." I applied the cream cheese liberally. "But I'm fine, Mom, so please don't worry. And today both Modesty and I are playing hooky. We're putting our works-in-progress on hold and going for a drive in the country. She'll be here about nine. Nice day for it, right?"

She filled my cup and frowned, causing vertical lines to form between her eyebrows. "Right. Jake, you have trouble lying to strangers; why would you try to deceive your own mother? If you'd tell me the truth, I'd worry easier."

Whatever the hell that meant. "There's no need to worry at all. We're taking a ride up to Westchester. Er . . . we might stop at Manhattanville . . . I'll show Modesty my alma mater . . . then . . . we'll . . . um . . . we'll stop in Tarrytown to visit Dr. Nujurian. If she's home, I'd like to ask her a few questions. Now you know our itinerary. Nothing for you to be concerned about, okay?"

"Unless the doctor serves you a suicide sandwich, spread with a mix of hemlock and toadstools, washed down with a cyanide chaser." My mother took a vicious bite out of her bagel. Then she put her lipstick-red, Ben Franklin reading glasses back on and stuck her nose into the style section.

Modesty called as I was blowing my hair. "The car isn't ready. The mechanic says he needs another ten or fifteen minutes. That's repairman-speak for the parts haven't arrived and the job will take at least an hour."

"Maybe not; keep the faith. We're still going, aren't we?"

"Yes, but I'll be there when I'm there."

I finished dressing and, with an unexpected gift of time, went to work. I like to outline each upcoming chapter on a legal pad. Then, when I hit the keys, the plot tends to move along. Most of the time. This *Heads Roll* manuscript had proved to be as difficult to draft in longhand as on the computer. When a ghostwriter detests her employer's protagonist and finds the story line repugnant, only the advance compels her to create. My current employer, an off-Broadway musical-comedy producer whose failures littered his résumé, came from a wealthy family who had supported his habit of backing turkeys. His main character, the chorus girl-killer, remained a one-dimensional horror show. Fortunately, I'd reached the final pages and the last musical murder. Sketching out the scene, I set the seventh sing-along site on the Circle Line, where an unsuspecting tourist loses his head to the raucous sounds of Rodgers and Hammerstein's "There Is Nothing Like a Dame."

Just as I was figuring out how the hapless homicide detective—not at all like Ben—would arrive on board to capture the killer chorus girl—maybe on a coastguard cutter?—my mother barged into my bedroom. She'd changed from her jogging suit to a smart three-piece, taupe tweed ensemble: a cropped jacket topping a matching vest and long, narrow skirt, worn with dark chocolate leather ankle boots. Her smart new hairstyle reminded me of Diane Sawyer's. "Jake, Ashley Butler's down in the lobby. She can't wait till tonight; she must speak to you immediately."

I hadn't heard the intercom. "Well, I guess you'd better ask her up." My feeling of euphoria, resulting from almost closing the book on *Heads Roll,* faded fast. What the hell did Ashley Butler want from me?

"Oh, there's something else," my mother said. There always was. "NBC just announced that Senator Fione will be waked at Campbell's tomorrow afternoon and evening. The viewing will be open to the public. First come; first in. The funeral will be held at St. Pat's on Wednesday at eleven A.M. The mass is by invitation only, as is the senator's farewell cruise around Manhattan, followed by his burial at sea."

Marveling at how my current fictional denouement tied into Charlie Fione's grand finale, I asked, "Has

Gypsy Rose arranged for us to be aboard that Ashes Away cruise? For the channeling, I mean? I know Ben plans on attending."

"Don't worry, darling, we both have boarding passes." My mother winked. I knew that she thrived on this opportunity to reverse roles and to show me up for fretting unnecessarily. "Ben Rubin will have to provide his own! And all the crime writers will receive invitations for both the viewing—no waiting on line—and for the service in the cathedral. Now I'll buzz your visitor in."

Mom served Ashley and me tea in the living room and went off to work. Joan Mazza would be signing her latest dreaming-your-own-reality workbook at Gypsy Rose's bookstore this morning and they were expecting a big crowd.

Ashley and I were seated in the Casablanca chairs, facing the windows that overlooked Ninety-second Street. While my unexpected guest fidgeted with her teacup, adding two teaspoons of sugar, stirring up a storm, then squeezing the slice of lemon as if she were ringing someone's neck, I checked out her incredible outfit. The navy-blue blazer, white cotton shirt, opened to show a lacy bit of bra, thigh-high, plaid miniskirt, kneesocks, and penny loafers reminded me of Barbie dressed in a grade-school uniform. Combined with this Lolita-like getup, Ashley's raccoon-ringed eyes, bloodred lips, and teased-to-the-rafters hair struck me as somewhat revolting. Of course, since I didn't like the lady, my judgment might be considered as harsh as her makeup.

She looked around, then pointing to the dentil molding, said, "This is such a comfy old shoe of a co-op and fairly large as a New York apartment's size and scale goes. As a country girl, raised on a plantation, I just can't get used to sharing space in a building with sixty other families. Kinda like being placed on a shelf, you know. And, mercy me, one that holds three other apartments beside mine! Have you all lived here long?"

"Most of my life and I love it." I could hear my teeth clench. "So, will you be returning to Tara and the land anytime soon?"

"Aren't you a sweet little thing, picturing me as Miss Scarlett O'Hara. She's the quintessential southern belle, don't you think? As well as your namesake! Though I must tell you, this is not the first time I've heard that comparison, Jake. *Gone With the Wind* is my very favorite book!"

"Look, Ashley, I have an appointment in a few minutes, could we move this along?"

"Well sure, sugar. We're on topic now. I want to talk to you about writing and there never has been a better writer than Miss Margaret Mitchell of Atlanta, Georgia, has there?"

Hemingway and Tolstoy came to mind, but I just said, "Go on."

"Dennis Kim certainly thinks mighty highly of you, Jake. Have you two been acquainted for some time?"

I didn't feel like playing twenty questions with Ashley Butler controlling the game. "More than twenty-five years, but can we please get to the reason for your visit?"

She pouted. "Dennis is representing my mystery novel, actually, at the late Senator Fione's suggestion. Pax Publishing has given me a tidy advance. The premise is darling—sweet-potato-pie appeal—kinda Harper Lee meets Truman Capote. As kids, they were neighbors in real life, did you know that?"

"Yes, I knew." I wondered where she was going with this and why Dennis hadn't mentioned a business connection to Charlie Fione.

"Well, Pax just loved the proposal and synopsis. And my editor said I had an amusing and intriguing opening chapter, describing it as playful as a frisky puppy. But now my promising puppy has turned into an old bitch. I can't get that dog's tail to wag. I'm in terminal writer's block, Jake. I need a ghost!"

Puzzled, I stared at her. If she'd ghosted all of Carita Magenta's color-me-comatose books, why would she suddenly need a ghost for her own project?

"Will you do it, Jake?" Ashley sounded as if her life depended on it. "There's a big advance and I'm prepared to be generous regarding royalties. Dennis says you're a great ghost, though, of course, he can't reveal what you've written. And that's one entertainment attorney who really knows this business, even if, in your case, he's more than a little prejudiced. You are aware that the gentleman's completely crazy about you, aren't you?"

Nineteen

As we drove across the seemingly endless span of the Tappan Zee Bridge, I marveled at the beauty of its structure and the magnificent view. The windows of the Volkswagen were wide open and the late-morning sun warmed my face as I stuck my head out to savor the scenery.

Modesty, after expressing revulsion at having been assaulted head-on by Ashley's hair as the latter had exited my lobby, remained unusually quiet. Her tiny features were set in an inscrutable but intriguing expression. The corners of her glossed but color-free lips had turned up in what might be considered a slight smile. And the glint that flickered in those pale green eyes hadn't been caused by the sunshine. If I didn't know how totally out of character it would be, I'd almost believe Modesty had a man on her mind.

Pulling myself away from the river, I took another look at her profile. "A dollar for your thoughts."

"A booming-economy joke, Jake? Not funny." Like

she'd laugh if it had been. "Here's what I'm thinking: Tarrytown is a big place and God only knows where Dr. Assisted Suicide's residence is located. I hope you can read a map. There's one in the glove compartment. See if you can find Heaven Scent Vista. Now, that's funny."

We passed several estates and the space between the mansions expanded when we turned onto a tree-hooded road. Even in mid-March, I could imagine how lush this lane would look from May through October. And how dangerous with ice on the trees in winter. I strained to read the calligraphy on a Victorian signpost a few feet ahead. "Dove Drive. Make a right here, Modesty. We go about a half mile, then turn left on Serenity Way. That should lead us straight to Heaven Scent Vista."

"This entire trip is a sick joke. What do you expect to learn from Dr. Deadly?"

Dove Drive was unpaved and the bug bounced in its ruts. "I told you—and this is just a hunch—if we ask the doctor the right questions, I think we'll get some answers. Maybe even find out more about those threatening letters. Something that will help prove Hunter didn't send them. And last night you agreed with my gut feeling that Edwina's scheduling Charlie's appointment with Dr. Nujurian has some connection, however tenuous, with his murder."

"I still do, or I wouldn't be here. But we don't have an appointment. Why should the doctor agree to see us?"

"I'll make sure that her nurse or receptionist lets the doctor know that we're suspicious. I'll even point out that instead of Senator Fione's keeping his date with the doctor tomorrow, we'll be attending his wake at Campbell's. That should get Nujurian's attention. Then, if nothing else, curiosity should entice her to talk to us."

"Not if she's the one who provided Edwina with the poison."

"Dr. N's assisted suicides are painless passings; cyanide is a rotten way to go. That's not the connection."

"What is?"

"Slow down. Make a left after the Christmas tree; that's Serenity Way. I don't know what the connection is, but I know there is one. The next right should be Heaven Scent Vista. Let's hope we have an awakening when we arrive there."

Two enormous blue spruces—at least sixty feet high—formed an arch, framing the entrance to Serenity Lane. Either one would have been a fine selection for this year's Christmas-tree-lighting ceremony at Rockefeller Center's skating rink.

As we drove through the natural gate, the path turned primitive. Ruts became furrows, fallen branches blocked our way, and mud from the recent rain splattered Modesty's whitewall tires. A castle on a hill loomed to our right. Veering away from the bramble, Modesty inched up a steep hill, our final destination confirmed by a large hand-lettered sign, posted on a tree: HEAVEN SCENT VISTA—KEEP OUT. Only the moat was missing.

A Norman Revival, too big to be merely a mansion and clearly intended to be a home its owner could call a castle, covered about half an acre. Its red-brick facade had touches of Tudor. I wondered if a Tower of Tarrytown, providing prison cells for the doctor's enemies, had been built in the backyard. Two big bronze lions stood guard in front of stone steps leading to massive, oak front doors. Under winged Gothic gargoyles, whose cruel eyes glared at all guests, dozens of ivy-twined turrets and high, tiny, wood-framed windows evoked images of Rapunzel letting her hair down. In lieu of a rose garden, a wrought-iron-gated cemetery covered most of the courtyard. Ancient marble angels topped many of the less-than-manicured graves' crumbling tombstones.

Modesty glanced from Dr. Nujurian's castle to the cemetery. "One-stop shopping?" My nervous laughter seemed loud enough to carry up the stone steps. The left door swung open. Jesus! Could that tinny titter really have penetrated the thick oak? A tall, skinny young man, with sparse, wren-brown hair, thick glasses, and the largest Adam's apple I've ever encountered, stood and silently stared out at us.

"We want to see the doctor. Is she in?" Modesty stared back and delivered her lines, using her icy-cold, I'm-a-longtime-practicing-Manhattan-eccentric-so-don't-believe-even-for-a-New-York-second-that-any-Ichabod-Crane-Sleepy-Hollow-type-hick-can-act-odder-than-I-do voice.

And it worked. The man said, "Dr. Nujurian is with a patient." God, could she be giving a lethal injection to someone as we spoke? "If you'll come in and state your reason for being here, when she finishes, I'll discuss it with her; however, the doctor never sees anyone without an appointment." Except for a narrow slit in his lips, hardly a muscle on his face moved.

The entrance hall could have been used as a ballroom. The ceiling was so high that the wide marble staircase seemed to be stretching to the sky. Requisite suits of armor lined one wall. Three long, narrow, rough-hewn oak benches, positioned below what appeared to be the entire Plantagenet family's portraits lined the other and continued up the wall behind the brass banister.

"Please follow me." The young man's lockjaw had to be congenital. We trailed behind him, deep into the belly of the beast, to another oak, floor-to-ceiling double door. He opened it and we entered a Cecil-Beaton-meets-Alfred-Hitchcock-and-creates-ye-olde-grand-Gothic-castle-movie-set design.

Frescoes on the ceiling featured pastel murals of a heaven where all the pleasingly plump cherubs had pale yellow wings spread over soft pink clouds, spun gold ringlets, rosy cheeks, and baby blue eyes. These contrasted sharply with the bronze, gargoyle-ugly heads of young women that had been placed, facedown—the better to startle the visitors—in each of the ceiling's four corners. The walls were covered with tapestries that seemed to recount some knightly tale of honor. There were six or seven groupings of furniture—enough to fill as many living rooms. We stood near the door in an area containing two peach satin French side chairs, a rust velvet settee, a gold brocade couch, and three oak tables. Oriental rugs, in shades of rust, blue, and peach, were scattered over the stone floor.

"Let me introduce myself," our host said, allowing himself a tight smile. "I'm Bartholomew Irving, Dr. Nujurian's assistant." He looked at us with great expectations.

Once again, Modesty lived up to them. Throwing away my proposed script, she improvised a far better one, with great dialogue.

"I'm Modesty Meade and this is an emergency, Mr. Irving." She placed an arm around me. "My sister, Jake is dying. Meanwhile, she lives in agony and we must see Dr. Nujurian today. We've been driving all night through hell and back. This is our last chance. Jake can't suffer through tomorrow without knowing the end is in sight."

I gasped and, unwittingly, played into Modesty's scenario. She shoved me into the nearest peach satin chair. "Sit down, sis." Then, glancing at me, she stage-whispered to Irving, "This is such a strange disease. Her color is good, but her liver is shot."

I sank into the chair, trying to look sick. Through half-closed eyes, I watched Bartholomew Irving's Adam's apple bob. "What's wrong with her?" He sounded like a man in the throes of sexual excitement. "Are you sure it's terminal?" His breath came in pants. No doubt about it, the possibility of my death was a turn-on.

Modesty took my wrist in her hand and felt my pulse. "She should have been gone weeks ago. This is too cruel. Jake used to be so alive, so attractive, so young. I wish you could have known her . . . before." Her voice broke. A Tony Award performance. "Do you realize that she's only eighteen, though she looks forty? The ravages of this deadly disease causes its victims to age rapidly!" If we pulled this off, I'd consider injecting Modesty with cyanide. "Please, Mr. Irving, go and tell Dr. Nujurian that we need to see her. Now!"

"Oh God!" Irving shuddered. And his breathing remained heavy. I hoped he didn't climax before we reached the next plateau. "She's with a patient, but if Jake can hold on for just a tad longer, I'll inform Dr. Nujurian that your sister is ready and waiting!"

With me leaning on Modesty, we slowly followed Mr. Irving out of the great room, across the huge entrance hall, to yet another enormous oak double door. This one led to an elegant reception area and beyond that the good doctor's office. Slumped on a settee, attempting to project pain, I thought, this has to be the goddamn cheeriest room I've ever seen. Yellow dominated, with lots of white and touches of blue. Crisp chintz and linen fabrics—their patterns combining the three colors—covered the overstuffed chairs and love seats. White and yellow daisies filled blue Ming vases. And beneath high, stone arches, glass doors let the sunshine in from a garden that had slate steps leading down to the river.

Modesty asked Bartholomew Irving to please fetch—I couldn't believe she actually used that verb—a glass of water as she thought I was about to faint. After he left, she totally lost it. "You should act sicker, you know." Sounding annoyed as hell. "How can I convince Dr. Nujurian that you want to commit suicide if your cheeks are so pink?" She thrust a tissue at me. "Here, wipe off that blush, then rub some of your mascara under your eyes. Haggard. That's the look I want. You need to appear haggard before you die."

"Jesus! I'm not wearing any blush." I decided it was definite. I was going to kill her. "If my cheeks are flushed, it's probably high blood pressure. You're making me nervous. Stop acting so weird. I think you're starting to believe that I really am dying."

"Just do it, Jake!" Modesty directed. "Don't question motivation."

Bartholomew Irving entered from the hall door, carrying a tall crystal glass of water and a small bucket of ice on a silver tray just as across the room, the door to the doctor's inner sanctum opened and a dead ringer for Doris Day, circa *Pillow Talk*, bounced in, chatting away to an elderly couple. Dr. Nujurian, I presumed. She even had the same catch in her voice as Doris's 1960s movie virgins. But what caught my attention—scaring me to death and causing me to jump up and to knock the tray out of Irving's hand, blowing my sick-and-dying act while spilling water on the Persian rug—were her patients. Standing tall, proud, and sad, beside the doctor, were my favorite Carnegie Hill neighbors, former babysitters, and dear old friends, Mr. and Mrs. Neal.

.

Twenty

Bartholomew Irving finally dropped his jaw, staring in total amazement at my miraculous recovery. "Put Tarrytown right up there with Lourdes!" I said, hopping over the broken glass, elbowing the doctor out of my way, and embracing the Neals.

"Who is this woman?" Dr. Nujurian's voice had lost the endearing Doris Day catch and become quite strident.

Mr. Neal kissed my cheek. "Why, Jake, what in the world are you doing here?"

"She's a charlatan!" Irving screamed as he knelt to mop up the mess that my unexpected recovery had left behind.

"You bloody idiot!" the doctor snarled.

"I'm so sorry, Dr. Nujurian!" Bartholomew Irving stammered, picking up the pieces of glass. "She really did appear to be dying."

"My prayers are answered!" Modesty said. "My sister is saved!" She sounded like the Reverend Kennedy, broadcasting from Fort Lauderdale on Sunday mornings. My mother sometimes squeezed him in between Tim Russert and Cokie Roberts. God only knows why. "Praise the Lord!" Modesty said. Then she joined my circle, giving both the Neals a big hug.

"I didn't know Jake and . . . er . . ." Mrs. Neal looked up at her husband.

"It's Modesty, dear." He smiled at his wife.

"Well, I didn't know Jake and Modesty were sisters. How nice for them," Mrs. Neal said. "This is an evil house, isn't it? Can we all leave now and go for a nice cup of tea at . . . er . . . at that place I like?"

"Sarabeth's," Modesty said. "Great idea, Mrs. Neal, Jake and I like it, too."

Desperate, I quickly tried to calculate where to go from here and decided that the only course of action left was a direct attack. But first I wanted to take care of my friends. "Mr. Neal, how did you get here?"

"The Amtrak, then a cab from the station." Visibly upset, Harry Neal shook his head. "Hell of a ride."

"Well, you're coming home with us." I turned to Modesty. "Please take the Neals to the car and stay with them until I'm finished here. I have some questions for the doctor. If I'm not out in fifteen minutes, call Ben Rubin."

"Now, just a minute," Dr. Nujurian began.

I gave her my sweetest smile. "Look, you either talk to me right now or I tell the police about those threatening letters you've been receiving"—which I had every intention of doing anyway—"and you can deal with them. Then I'd bet the district attorney might be interested to learn that you've been soliciting suicides while out on bail. But first, scratch the Neals from your list of patients." I hissed this last sentence into her face, actually, wanting to spit.

"We'll talk in my office. Follow me!" Dr. Nujurian ordered as Modesty led the Neals out. Doris Day playing doctor was history; a bitchy Bette Davis had replaced her.

The old oak desk had to be six feet across. The doctor's whimsical choice of decor—Steuben-glass angel mobiles, Jessie Wilcox Smith prints, and several vases filled with fresh yellow roses—must have been intended to uplift the spirits of her potential assisted-suicide patients. But the total picture, repeating the reception room's yellow, white, and blue color scheme, made me want to throw up.

"Sit down!" The doctor pointed to a comfy chintz chair in front of her desk, then sat in the swivel chair behind her desk. "Okay, who the hell are you and how do you know about those letters? Did you send them?"

"No. And neither did Hunter Green."

She laughed. The dullest laugh I'd ever heard. Devoid of any warmth or humor. "Did Hunter hire you? Are you a private investigator?"

"Just a friend . . . who knows him well enough to be certain that he never wrote them. Now listen up, Doctor. I watched two people die from cyanide poisoning a few days ago. An ugly end. The police think Hunter may be a double murderer. But I believe that the real killer may have sent you those letters as a red herring."

"Really?" She shoved a file to the far right side of the desk. "I can assure you that Hunter Green had a motive for killing Holly Halligan. He held her—and I might add me—responsible for his wife's death. For God's sake, he threatened Holly in front of Angela's mourners. And now he's after me. No one dislikes law enforcement's

ongoing invasion of individual rights more than I, but
for once, the cops are correct."

"Exactly what do these letters threaten, Dr. Nujurian?"

"Mostly they're filled with accusations." She tapped
her pink nails on the desktop as if she were typing. "All
innuendo. No substance. The writer wants me punished
for helping humanity. Twisting my life's work to suit
his warped viewpoint. There's not a tangible shred of
evidence in any of them."

"So, was there another letter in today's mail?"

"Yes. But why do you ask that? How could you know
how many letters have arrived? Did Hunter tell you that
he'd mailed a third one?"

I ignored her questions. "Do these threats also connect
you to Senator Fione's death?" A wild guess. But my
words made the doctor look sick. Nujurian reached for
the file she'd pushed to the side, but I moved faster and
snatched it first. Three envelopes fell from the folder to
the floor. Dr. Nujurian picked up a letter opener, then
shot out of her seat and around the desk in a flash, but
not before I'd grabbed the envelopes. The block-printed
address, written in red crayon, caught my attention. That
type of printing—warning me to butt out—had been
used on the bucket of red paint. I read one of the post-
marks. Murray Hill. The very same neighborhood where
Carita Magenta's purple bathtub served as her kitchen's
focal point. As Dr. Nujurian lurched at me, brandishing
the letter opener, the envelopes went flying. I kicked her
shin as hard as I could and she fell to her knees. Her
screams brought Bartholomew Irving barging into the
office. I figured my fifteen minutes were almost up. If I
didn't leave now, Modesty might call Ben. I didn't want
that. While Irving ran to the doctor's aid, I hurried to
the door. But I couldn't leave without an exit line. Look-

ing over my shoulder, I saw that Nujurian and Irving were both on their knees. She was shoving the letters back into the file while he still appeared to be begging for forgiveness.

"Good-bye, Dr. Nujurian," I said with great enthusiasm. "I do hope to see you aboard the senator's Ashes Away cruise on Wednesday. We're channeling Charlie Fione from the world beyond; maybe he'll have a message for you."

. . . . .

Marianne Neal dozed as we started the trip back to Manhattan. But Harry Neal, extremely agitated, berated himself. "How could I have been so callow? And cowardly. I'm ashamed of myself. But I didn't have any hope."

"Mr. Neal, why didn't you come to us?" I asked, turning to face him in the backseat. God, what a mess! I felt sad. Powerless. Frustrated. "You know, no matter how bad things get, Mom and Gypsy Rose, somehow, find a way to help."

"I was desperate, Jake. Scared. There didn't seem to be another solution . . . and that Holly Halligan was one fast talker. If it were only Marianne's problem, I would have taken care of her till the end, but I've been feeling weaker and weaker. Then, two weeks ago, I was diagnosed with heart failure. I'm not afraid to die, Jake, but I can't leave Marianne behind." A tear rolled down his wrinkled cheek. I could see Modesty, wiping her eyes, as we drove out of Tarrytown.

She blew her nose, took a deep breath, and said, "Mr. Neal, you're not going to die immediately. I had an uncle with heart failure. He outlived the cardiologist who said he'd be dead in a year." Blunt Modesty could be spouting the right stuff. Certainly, I couldn't think of a goddamn thing to say. "Furthermore," she continued, "I'll bet that whatever you paid for that Ashes Away cruise and Dr. Nujurian's double-whammy needle would be more than enough for home health care round-the-clock. Then you and Mrs. Neal could stay together. It won't be easy. Sometimes, life really does suck. You're not a quitter, Mr. Neal, and you two could have a lot of good days ahead of you. And we'll all be there for you. Isn't that right, Jake?"

Totally straight-thinking logic there. A much better solution than I—or, maybe, even Mom and Gypsy Rose—could have come up with. Mr. Neal patted Modesty on the shoulder and gave me a weak smile.

"That's a grand plan, Modesty!" I said. "Of course we'll be there, Mr. Neal. You can count on it. Now, you and Mrs. Neal are having dinner with Mom, Modesty, and me tonight." I reached for my cell phone. "But first I'm calling Gypsy Rose to ask her to cook something special. Roast chicken and mashed potatoes. Perhaps she'll bake her buttermilk biscuits, too. Oh, and string-bean casserole. Mom can handle that. Then I'm calling Dennis Kim to see what he can do about getting your money back. Since he's Holly Halligan's executor, that shouldn't be a problem. He can just take it out of her estate! I'll ask him and Mr. Kim over for dinner, too. Dennis can bring the white wine."

"Are we in Hawaii yet?" Mrs. Neal asked.

Twenty-one

Dinner was a great success, but dessert was postponed because of death. And I'd been really looking forward to Gypsy Rose's peach cobbler. She'd just put it in the oven to warm when the phone rang. My head was in the freezer, searching for the Edy's French vanilla. "Ben—for you, Jake," Gypsy Rose said as she lined up the Waterford dessert dishes and I emerged triumphant, placing the ice cream on the counter to soften. Mom kept the freezer as crowded as if she actually cooked and colder than Antarctica.

One of Ben's more endearing qualities is cutting to the chase. "Carita Magenta's dead," he said. "Murdered in her purple bathtub."

Macabre visions of Marat and Charlotte Corday flooded my mind. "Murdered! Jesus! How? Did someone stab her?"

"No. Why would you say that?"

"I don't know why. Sorry, my imagination went wild there for a moment," I said as Gypsy Rose turned off the oven, covered the cobblers in tin foil, and stuck the ice cream back into the freezer. "What did happen?"

"The actual cause of death was drowning. The killer held her head underwater. I don't understand why Magenta kept that old tub in the middle of her kitchen—boy, that's one colorful room, looks like an explosion in a crayon box—she never took a bath in it, that's for sure. She wouldn't have fit."

"So I heard. A couple of days ago Modesty went to Carita's to discuss having her aura aligned. She filled me in about the tiny, old-fashioned, purple tub and the rest of the bizarre color scheme. When she'd visited the apartment, Venus DeMill had been soaking in a bubble bath. Modesty's convinced that Carita and Venus have been—er—quite close for years."

"Yeah." Ben sounded tired. And distant. "Well, DeMill discovered the body. Apparently, she spends several days a week at Magenta's. Anyway, her screams brought a neighbor, a Mrs. Samuels, running to Carita's apartment. Samuels found the door open. Venus had collapsed in a heap on that god-awful orange-and-green linoleum. The neighbor called 911. DeMill is currently under a doctor's care at Maurice Welch's."

"Ben, Carita Magenta was a big woman, wouldn't it have been difficult for the killer to have held her head underwater long enough to drown her? Seems to me that would have required a lot of strength," I said, wondering if Wanda Sparks, Ashley Butler, or Edwina Carrington Fione would have been powerful enough. Even Venus DeMill, who was tall and appeared to be very muscular, might have had trouble holding Carita down. "Isn't it more likely that the murderer is a man?"

"A cast-iron frying pan was found on the floor, next to the tub. And there's a bump on the back of Carita's head. Looks like the killer bopped her one before drowning her. So I guess the field's wide open. However, there is an arrest warrant being written out for a man as we speak."

"Who!" My loud question startled Gypsy Rose, who stood by the stove, unabashedly eavesdropping.

"Rickie Romero!" Ben said with satisfaction. "Another neighbor—who'd recognized him from TV and the tabloids—spotted him leaving Carita's apartment about fifteen minutes before Mrs. Samuels heard DeMill's screams. And he never showed up this afternoon for his meeting with his parole officer."

"Does that mean Hunter Green's no longer a suspect?" I asked. Gypsy Rose nodded encouragingly.

"Not for this murder. His alibi's airtight. Joe Cassidy and I were searching Green's loft while he groused long and loud, during the time frame when Carita died. That doesn't let him off the hook for the Senator and Holly Halligan."

"For God's sake, Ben, hasn't it occurred to you that Carita's drowning has to be connected to the poisonings?" I shouted. "That the same person has to be responsible!"

"And hasn't it occurred to you that Hunter Green and Rickie Romero may be partners in crime? Under the guise of Hunter providing literary advice to Rickie, while he was writing his novel in jail, their mutual greed—fueled by the Faith diamond—could have turned them into unlikely co-conspirators. Then they both had major motives for wanting Holly Halligan dead, didn't they?"

Jesus! He had me there! That was one plot twist I hadn't even considered. But . . . of course . . . damn . . .

it did seem plausible. "But what about Senator Fione? Why would they both want—"

"Come on, Jake! You've been digging up the dirt over on Tenth Avenue, haven't you?" Ben's voice had turned icy. "You must have stumbled onto a Rickie Romero/ Charlie Fione connection."

While I had what I considered hard evidence about a long-ago link between the Fione family and Holly Halligan, I only harbored a strong hunch regarding any past history between Charlie Fione and Rickie Romero. What had Ben unearthed? Maybe, if I handled this right, I could find out.

"Now, consider this an official warning." Ben spoke softly, his voice still ice-cold. "Stop interfering in this investigation, Jake. I don't want your mother to find you dead in the bathtub. Or poisoned in the kitchen. Even when we take Romero into custody, there could still be another killer on the loose out there. You and the ghosts are off this case. Effective immediately. Is that understood?" He hung up.

Jeez! I not only didn't learn any more about Fione and Romero, I never had a chance to ask for an update on Wanda Sparks's break-in. Given Ben's current attitude, I might never have that chance.

. . . . .

The peach cobbler tasted flat and Edy's usually robust flavor seemed to have faded, but Gypsy Rose and I managed to serve dessert and coffee without letting any of our table mates knowing that its delay had been caused by the news of Magenta's murder. Once Mom heard about Carita, she'd insist that I stay home, so I made Gypsy Rose promise to wait until after Modesty and I were out of there before she told my mother and

Dennis. Then I'd tell Modesty when we joined the other ghosts. Mr. Kim offered to see the Neals downstairs to their apartment and Mom and Gypsy Rose started to clear the table.

Thanking Gypsy Rose and Mom for hosting dinner two nights in a row, Modesty and I left Dennis to the ladies—risking that they'd probably have arranged my engagement by the time I returned home—and, ignoring Ben's warnings, grabbed a cab down to Too Tall Tom's. I could easily justify my actions. After all, the ghosts had completed their day's detecting, so why not listen to their results? And Modesty would sulk big time if she couldn't brag about improvising my near-fatal illness during our visit to Dr. Assisted Suicide.

When we arrived at Too Tall Tom's Christopher Street jewel of an apartment, Jane, giddy with excitement and flushed from downing two glasses of wine while waiting for us, insisted that she report first. That would mean postponing the delivery of my own news about Carita's murder, but anticipating the gratification of one-upping Jane, I graciously acquiesced.

"Donald Jay is a dreadful human being," Jane began. "Posing as a writer proved to be the perfect ploy; that man lives to read his and his bloody Crime Writers' press coverage. He'd perform sex acts in Brentano's window if he thought it would draw more of a crowd to his conference. I think he's thrilled that Holly and Senator Fione died on one of his panels, and despite Jay's protestations to the contrary, he's convinced even bad publicity is good publicity. With a little flattery, he revealed his top choice for killer."

"Who?" I asked.

"Rickie Romero. Because A—he inherits Holly's estate. And B—Jay says Rickie had a longstanding grudge against Senator Fione. Guess what, my fellow ghosts?" Jane paused, tapping her wineglass on Too Tall Tom's Hepplewhite table, eliciting a cross look from our host.

"What?" Modesty and I asked as one.

"Though Jay wouldn't elaborate, I figured out that the Fione/Romero conflict had something to do with Plattsburgh!" Jane sat back, like Perry Mason, waiting for the jury's reaction to her revelation.

"How did you deduce that and what, if any, evidence do you have?" Modesty asked, sounding underwhelmed.

"I questioned Jay about his land in Plattsburgh and Senator Fione's opposition to the federal government's using it. You know, trying to reinforce Jay's motive." Jane had gone on the defensive, giving her summation. "He wouldn't discuss either his property there or the now-postponed Senate vote that could leave him penniless. But Jay did hint that Romero's Plattsburgh's roots were connected to his motive for murdering Charlie Fione!" At best, Jane's argument was based on hearsay and her own speculation, but Ben had presented his case against Rickie earlier, and I suspected she might be right.

"I don't think Rickie Romero killed anyone," Modesty snapped. "Jane, you're no Perry Mason. Not even a second-rate Della Street."

"Hey, don't be so sure about that!" I related the story of Ben's dessert-stopping phone call and finished, dramatically, with Rickie Romero's being on the loose and the police issuing an arrest warrant for him in connection with Carita Magenta's murder.

Modesty's pale eyes watered, and she fumbled in her big black bag for a tissue and blew her nose. Jane, annoyed at being topped, took no notice. But Too Tall

Tom, looking concerned and puzzled, refilled Modesty's glass. Jeez! How could I have been so dense? Like a blast of thunder, it dawned on me that, indeed, a man had been on Modesty's mind this morning. What else? Of all the men, in all of Manhattan, she'd fallen for our prime suspect: Rickie Romero. Where and when had he stolen her heart?

The moment passed, and Modesty managed to rearrange her features into their usual scowl. Before Jane could question her response, Too Tall Tom smiled and said, "My turn! I spent most of the morning with Venus DeMill. I'm still recovering! And I guess when that big hunk of woman finished with me, she went on to discover Carita's body."

"Did you learn anything new from her?" I asked, cutting into the Brie and spreading some on a cracker that I handed to Modesty. She accepted it, but glared at me.

"Oh, my dear, yes! And thanks to Venus, I'm more convinced than ever that Maurice is our man," Too Tall Tom answered me while smiling at Modesty.

"Why?" Jane asked. "Did she confirm that her fiancé is the killer?"

"If Venus weren't such a Viking, I'd swear she was the leprechaun who carried the cyanide-spiked beer to the panel. She's too big for the role, but I'd bet the Brie she helped Maurice plan the murders." Too Tall Tom took a huge hunk of his wager and wolfed it down.

"Surely, she didn't aid and abet the murder of her dear, old friend Carita!" I said. "You can't believe that, can you?"

"Brush up your Brutus, Jake." Too Tall Tom rolled his *r*s. "Venus wouldn't be the first Roman to betray her best chum."

"But . . . why would she?" I asked.

"Well, maybe Carita accused Venus's intended. The ammunition was there. You see, in addition to Maurice's motives for killing Rickie Romero and Holly Halligan, it seems he also had a motive for killing Senator Fione," Too Tall Tom said.

"What?" Modesty rejoined the fray.

"Maurice Welch had been Charlie Fione's ghost! The brain behind *Death of a Filibuster*. He not only didn't receive his promised co-author credit on the cover, the senator stiffed him on the six-figure fee!"

Twenty-two

"Now, let's see if I've gotten this straight," my mother said. "Wanda was Rickie's ghost; Maurice Welch was Senator Fione's ghost; Ashley, or, possibly, Wanda was Carita's ghost; now Ashley wants you to be her ghost. Can that be right? It sounds like a Noël Coward farce."

I laughed. "It sure does. But if all we've been told—including Venus DeMill's latest flash to Too Tall Tom—has been the truth, and I wouldn't count on that, your summation is on the money."

We were having a late breakfast. Big enough to fortify us for the senator's wake this afternoon. Scrambled eggs, garnished with ketchup and only slightly singed on the edges, English muffins, toasted to perfection—a first—and served with Gypsy Rose's homemade raspberry preserves, copious cups of tea, and, for each of us, a sliver of leftover peach cobbler that Mom had warmed up in the oven.

There were several items on my long list of suspicions

and questions that I wanted to ask Dennis about; I'd left a message at his office. Meanwhile, I had my own resident resource—with more than a half century of reading murder mysteries, honing her naturally devious mind, illogical logic, and great eye for details—sitting next to me. I knew Mom loved to play armchair detective with me. She only got testy when I tried to take the game outside our house, violating her self-imposed safety zone.

I poured another cup of tea and began. "Why would Rickie want Carita dead? I know she'd spewed venom at him for creating two characters, based on her and Venus DeMill, but Rickie has denied that charge, insisting that *Cat on Trump Tower's Roof* is total fiction. And even if those characters were thinly veiled versions of Carita and Venus, what's the big deal? This is the twenty-first century. Who cares what two women writers and a drop-by cat burglar did or didn't do to entertain each other?"

"Perhaps Rickie had another reason for killing her," my mother said. "Remember, in the book, the thief slips up, letting the Carita character know where his jewels are stashed. If that's true, and Rickie's on the prowl, Venus could be his next victim."

"Jeez, Mom! Speaking of where the jewels might be stashed reminds me of something else. Ben thinks that Rickie and Hunter may be in this together. Hunter himself admitted to me that when he was hanging around Rickie's cell, he found out where the Faith diamond was hidden, so Ben—"

"You can't possibly believe that Hunter Green would have helped Rickie poison Holly Halligan and Senator Fione, can you!" My mother jostled her cup and some tea spilled onto her saucer.

"No." I sighed. "However, Hunter did have a major motive for killing Holly Halligan. He even threatened her in front of all those witnesses at Angela's funeral! I can understand where Ben's coming from . . ." As a look of horror filled my mother's face, I quickly added, "That doesn't mean I agree with him!"

"Well, I shouldn't think so!" Mom said, then switched gears. "How about Maurice Welch? As crazy as it sounds, could he have killed Carita to eliminate his competition for Venus's favors?"

"Do you realize that Maurice is the only suspect who had three motives, one for each member of the poisoned panel? He wanted Romero dead, because of what he perceived as *Cat on Trump Tower's Roof*'s attack on Carita and Venus . . . and he had no reason to suspect that Rickie didn't drink—"

"Can you be certain about that?"

I shrugged. "No, I can't. Rickie was locked up in a cell, and they weren't serving cocktails there. After he was released, who knows? Maybe, no one—including the killer—ever noticed that Romero didn't drink. What we do know is this: In addition to avenging Venus DeMill's honor by killing Rickie, Maurice had two motives for murdering Holly Halligan. She broke his young heart, and in his old age, she screwed him out of a small fortune for his future Ashes Away voyage. And according to Venus, Senator Fione welshed on Welch—twice— first on his co-author credit on *Death of a Filibuster*'s cover, then on his more-than-half-million-dollar ghost-writing fee."

"Why haven't the police shown more interest in Welch? Or Wanda? Or, even, Edwina Fione?"

"That's a good question, Mom. Tunnel vision, I guess. Ben set his aim on Rickie Romero that first day in the

Plaza ballroom, and no matter what other suspects jump into his crosshairs, Ben can't see them. Last night he seemed bound and determined to prove that Hunter was Rickie's accomplice."

"A case certainly could be made against Rickie. Minus Hunter! That cat burglar has always been a lone wolf; and now he's gone undercover."

"And I'm afraid to even contemplate just whose cover that big, bad wolf could be hiding under—"

"Good God, Jake! Why do you say that? Who are you talking about? Where? You have to tell Ben. Now! I won't have you aiding and abetting an accused killer. If you have any idea where Romero is . . . we—" The intercom buzzer interrupted my mother. "Modesty and Too Tall Tom are on their way up."

In what had to be a true measurement of my mother's concern, she greeted Modesty and Too Tall Tom still wearing her flannel bathrobe, fuzzy slippers, and a naked face. Mom ordered me to put the kettle on while she frantically filled the ghosts in on our sleuth session and spread raspberry jam on their English muffins. Well aware that one muffin wouldn't make a dent in Too Tall Tom's appetite, I stuck four more in the toaster oven.

"Jake's just about to call Ben and tell him where she suspects Rickie Romero may be bedded down!" Mom finished her recap.

Modesty's heavy gold chain held the thickest cross I've ever seen. And the widest. It covered most of her chest. Where had this hunk of gold come from? It must have cost a fortune. I marveled that carrying all that weight, she could stand up straight. At Mom's words, Modesty twisted the chain, but then seemed to stand taller than her sixty-two inches. Her pale green eyes, flickering with fury, met mine.

"Oh no!" I said. "Nancy Drew went out of control there for a moment, Mom. I don't really have any thoughts on where Rickie Romero might be." My mother shot me a look of disbelief. But before she could cross-examine me, I rambled on, "Or any other bright ideas, for that matter . . . so, if you guys have—"

Too Tall Tom jumped in. "That's exactly why Modesty and I are here, bright-eyed, bushy-tailed, and chock-full of theories that must be discussed before we leave for the wake. Think of all those potential murders, dropping by to say their last good-byes to Senator Fione. Why, this afternoon, Campbell's Funeral Home will turn into a veritable playing field, filled with killer action! And our team needs to be at the top of our game."

Our strategy was severely hampered by our conflicting positions on whodunit. And why. We were all over the place. And all over each other. Everyone did agree on one point: Carita Magenta's murder had been connected to—and a direct result of—the poisonings.

"I was so sure that the now departed Carita had sent those threatening letters to Dr. Nujurian!" I said. "The Murray Hill postmark, those messages scrawled in crayon, all of it seemed to tie in with the printing used on the bucket of paint that just missed coloring me red." I shook my head. "Do you think the letters and the pail were only magenta herrings?" Too Tall Tom laughed and Modesty almost smiled.

Too Tall Tom started on his second English muffin, third theory, and was pouring himself a freshly brewed cup of the gourmet coffee that he'd brought along with him, knowing ours was a tea-drinking house, when Jane arrived.

Her well-honed organizational skills, as well as her smart, new Ellen Tracey navy wool suit, were very much in evidence as she handed out sheets of computer-generated graphs, with color-coded lines, dots, checks, and stars and bars, each color representing one of our suspects. Printed in bold, black letters across the top of the graph were the words MOTIVE, OPPORTUNITY, and MEANS. Jane's presentation looked as professional as a Dow Jones corporation's stock report. And as complicated.

Too Tall Tom served Jane a cup of coffee and I offered to share my graph with Mom, but she glanced at the kitchen clock and shrieked, "My God, it's almost noon, I have to start getting dressed!" Since the wake started at two and Mom's toilette could run up to ninety minutes, I assured her we'd clean up the kitchen.

Then, taking charge, Jane explained that the chart only reflected the poisonings, not the drowning, but any of the seven colorful suspects could have killed Carita. Who, why—and what—Magenta might have known remained blank.

We went to work. Jane pointed out the color-coordinated-to-suspect vertical lines and the matching bars, located at the bottom of the graph, that addressed the sum of our combined evidence, suspicions, observations, questions, and/or suppositions.

As instructed, we began with the blue line: Wanda Sparks. Under "Motive," Wanda had two stars. Going down to her first blue bar, we read: *1) As an unrequited admirer and an uncredited ghost, Wanda wanted to murder Rickie Romero and was willing to sacrifice Holly Halligan and the senator.* Jane's note: *Lame! Don't buy into this theory for a minute. 2) Wanda still loved Romero, though he'd pushed her out of his heart and off his book's cover.*

Jane's questions: *A) Was Wanda unaware that the*

beer contained cyanide? B) Or, knowing that Rickie would inherit Holly's estate, an accomplice to murder? C) Could Wanda have staged her own robbery? D) If not, what evidence connecting RR to HH was in those papers? Was there any motive for either Rickie Romero or Wanda to kill the senator? Other than some rumored long-ago connection between RR and Charlie Fione? Jane's conclusion: *Some version of motive # 2 might fly.*

Under "Opportunity," Jane had entered a big bold blue check. Her observations: *YES! Wanda could have been the leprechaun. She claimed she'd been in bathroom—changing into costume?—but neither Carita, Venus, nor Ashley spotted her there. Of course, Wanda said that she hadn't seen any of them, either.* "Means" received another big blue check. Jane's supposition: *See "Opportunity." If Wanda was the leprechaun, she transported the cyanide to the panelists. Notes: If Wanda worked with Rickie, he probably provided the poison. Same theory would apply if Wanda served as any other suspect's accomplice.*

"Jane, this is great!" I said. "Puts it all in perspective." Too Tall Tom agreed, and suggested that we complete the graph, before beginning any lengthy discussion. Modesty said nothing.

We moved on to the color purple. Edwina Carrington Fione. I wondered how Jane had chosen the color for each suspect. There wasn't too much evidence to raise the bar on Senator's Fione's widow. Yes, she'd arranged his Ashes Away cruise—had been overheard, saying how thrilled she'd been about it—and her husband's appointment with Dr. Assisted Suicide . . . but wanting, or wishing, someone dead didn't make you a murderer. The senator's mysterious, long-ago connection to Holly Halligan provided Edwina with a motive. But nothing you could take to court. Jane had entered a plump purple question mark under "Motive." And based on my re-portage—I'd sat right across the aisle from her and Mrs. Fione never left her seat—Jane concluded that if Edwina had poisoned the panel, she had an accomplice.

Orange, representing Donald Jay, Jane's favorite for killer—though last night, she seemed to be tilting toward Romero, while acknowledging that Jay himself had shoved her in that direction—bounced around the chart. An orange check mark next to the word *greed* appeared under "Motive." Jane's strong suspicion: Jay wanted to stop Charlie Fione from killing the waste-management bill, so he killed the senator. Holly and Rickie had the bad luck of being assigned to the wrong panel. Jane had serious questions regarding Jay's relationship with Rom-ero. Maybe Donald wanted him dead, too. He'd certainly tried to pin the murders on Rickie. Under "Opportunity," Jane cited an accomplice. Wanda, or Ashley, or some other flunky had played the part of leprechaun and served the cyanide. Possibly not knowing the beer had been spiked and that he—or she—had been the "Means" to murder.

"The leprechaun was afraid to come forward, but that same theory would apply if the leprechaun had been Welch's little helper," Too Tall Tom said, sneaking in his favorite suspect.

"Fear," Jane agreed. "Scared that the police wouldn't believe her—or him—but, in this scenario, more fright-ened of Donald Jay's wrath."

Hunter, of course, was green. And, unfortunately, so was much of the graph. The man had major "Motives" for murder: revenge and greed. Holly Halligan had not only conned his wife into an Ashes Away cruise, she'd arranged Angela's assisted suicide. And with Rickie

Romero dead, Hunter could retrieve the Faith diamond. As I followed the multiple green lines, stars, bars, dots, and check marks, I wondered where that diamond was hidden. Somehow, I sensed this information could be important. Jane's dire conclusions concurred with homicide's. While someone else had carried the cyanide, much of the evidence pointed to Hunter as the killer.

Red, however, ran rampant. Maurice. The man with three "Motives:" one per panelist. All of Jane's conclusions, as Mom's and mine had done earlier, reinforced Too Tall Tom's suspicions. And he also held to his position that Maurice—or Venus—had murdered Carita.

But Rickie Romero's black lines also led to guilt. Inheriting Holly Halligan's estate. Now, there was a "Motive"! And his not drinking, how convenient was that? Then his ties to Hell's Kitchen and a reported Romero/Fione Plattsburgh connection could uncover a second motive. Jane's summary was terse: *Review second theory for Wanda.*

Venus DeMill's buttercup yellow—an eerie choice, considering Carita had informed Modesty that Venus had a yellow aura, and Modesty had mentioned her yellow toenails—appeared in far too few places to make her a serious contender. No known "Motive" for killing any of the panelists, except Rickie, and that would have to be considered a long shot. No "Opportunity." Venus had been in the ladies' room with Carita earlier, but had been seated behind me when the leprechaun delivered the lethal potion. No visible "Means." Of course, as with any of the suspects, someone could have carried the poison for her. So, despite Too Tall Tom's belief that Venus was capable of killing Carita, Jane summarized the yellow readout re her poisoning the panel: *Not likely.*

Then Modesty finally spoke. "Two questions have occurred to me. Could Carita have recognized the leprechaun in the ladies' room? And if so, had she told Venus who it was?" None of us had an answer for either question.

Lavender was last. Representing Ashley. Pretty slim pickings. No "Motive" for murdering any of the three panelists. However, she certainly did have the "Opportunity." Ashley claimed that she'd been locked in a stall, suffering the pangs of food poisoning—and one couldn't miss the irony there—while the leprechaun was front and center; but no one could confirm her alibi. Yet with no motive, it didn't appear that Ashley had worked solo, and if she'd been another suspect's accomplice, who—and why—remained questions. Jane's bottom line: *Can't connect the dots.*

Just as the ghosts, with the possible exception of Modesty, were ready to dive in and dissect Jane's report, my mother came dashing into the kitchen. She looked great. All done up in basic black Donna Karan, with suede pumps and bag and the Franklin Mint's copy of Jackie Kennedy's much-photographed pearls. Noting her perfect makeup and hair, I knew too much time had gone by. "Jake! It's twenty after one. ANN is showing the mourners arriving at Campbell's and you're still in your bathrobe!"

Twenty-three

Beating my personal-best time, I was dressed and ready to leave for the wake in fifteen fast-paced minutes. Since Mom had popped in and out, having a snit when I wouldn't wear my own DKNY "good black dress," which she'd just pressed, and instead selected a wool pantsuit, "totally inappropriate for viewing a dead senator," I regarded this record toilette as a major victory.

Too Tall Tom, bless him, finished cleaning up the kitchen and went downstairs to hail two cabs. Not an easy assignment. The rest of us were almost out the door, when the phone rang.

"Don't answer that!" my mother said.

"It might be Dennis and I need to talk to him. You go on ahead with Modesty and Jane. I'll share the second cab with Too Tall Tom." As I ran back to my bedroom, I yelled over my shoulder, "What about Gypsy Rose? How will she get there?"

"She has a book signing at two, she'll meet us at

Campbell's after it's over," my mother said. "Gypsy Rose would have had one of the assistant sorceresses introduce the author, but it's that famous southern writer—you know—the one who always wears an old-fashioned white suit."

"Tom Wolfe!" I shouted as I picked up the phone.

"No! No! What's-his-name? Tom somebody else!" she shouted back. "Oh yes, I remember now. Tom Finn Sawyer—the guy who claims to be the reincarnation of Mark Twain!" I heard the door slam behind her.

"Sorry to disappoint you, Jake, but this isn't Tom Wolfe. Or even Mark Twain, calling from the world beyond," Dennis said. "However, if it will impress you and your mother, I'll spring for a white suit."

"Look, Dennis, I have no time to chat. We're late for the wake! Aren't you going?"

"Yes, later. I'm in court, but I'll be finished here in about thirty minutes. When I checked in with my office, my secretary said you'd called. What's up?"

"Something's been nagging me. About Holly Halligan. Mom says she came from upstate. The Catskills? And that she'd learned to ski at Grossinger's and an MGM talent scout discovered her on their slopes. Her first husband was a ski instructor. Is that right?"

"Maura O'Hara is, as usual, absolutely correct. Holly, herself, told me that she'd lived in Leeds, a small town in the Catskills. She worked as a waitress at Grossinger's, then fell in love with a ski instructor, and the sport, too. Funny you should ask. Just this morning, while reviewing her documents, I discovered that though Holly had lived in Leeds, she was born in a town called Au Sable Forks."

"I never heard of it."

"Well, it's just south of Plattsburgh." Dennis quietly

dropped his bomb, then waited in silence for my reaction.

"Jesus, Mary, and Joseph!"

Dennis laughed. "They may be the only three people who aren't connected to Plattsburgh. Should I tell Ben or do you want to?"

My head hurt. "I will . . . but not until after the wake. If Donald Jay is there, I want to have a chat with him first."

"Well, don't be guilty of obstructing justice, Jake. I'll see you at Campbell's." Dennis hung up.

Mrs. McMahon, who owned the co-op across from the Neals, waylaid me in the hall. Mom and I were convinced that our nosy neighbor had to be the busiest busybody in New York City.

"Going to the wake, Jake?" It didn't take a mystery-writing ghost to deduce that Mrs. M, draped in black crepe, her hair teased into a helmet, carrying her ratty Persian-lamb jacket in one hand and a Mass card in the other, planned on paying her own condolence call. Visiting the dead was her avocation. She never missed any funeral or wake within our zip code, unless the obit specified "family only."

"Yes. And I'm running late." I scooted past her. It wasn't very gracious, but I wanted—at any cost—to avoid sharing a cab with this harpy.

"My daughter, the Mary Kay district manager, is picking me up in her pink Cadillac. You never know, Patricia Ann might meet some prospective new customers at the viewing. She's the company's number-one sales star . . . across the entire United States! Won a trip to Las Vegas! But, what with you being a ghost, your profession has no recognition like that, does it?"

"No recognition," I agreed, opening the door.

"Why do you suppose Senator Fione's wake isn't being held at the Capitol Rotunda? I guess he just wasn't important enough."

I let myself be suckered in. "Mrs. Fione wanted the viewing to be local. So the people of New York could say good-bye. If he'd been laid out in Washington, you would have missed all the fun, wouldn't you, Mrs. McMahon?" I was out the door before she could answer.

The taxi driver, vexed at being kept waiting, first cursed at me in an exotic accent then drove like a madman, aiming for a smashup. His current target was the Fifth Avenue bus that blocked our left turn. When we missed its rear end by inches, I screamed. "Slow down, you'll get us all killed!"

He sped up and, dodging a Range Rover, placed a sidewalk vendor, selling his books from a kiosk too close to the curb, in peril.

A mounted policeman blew his whistle, but our driver, ignoring him and my entreaties, ran a red light and continued on down the avenue at a speed faster than my rapidly rising heart rate. The brutal pace made conversation impossible. Too Tall Tom appeared ashen. When unexpected gridlock forced the driver to stop at the intersection between Eighty-sixth Street and Fifth Too Tall Tom unbuckled his seat belt, opened the door, jumped out into the stalled traffic, and reached for my hand. Without paying the fare, we quickly zigzagged between the cars, heading for the east side of Fifth, as the driver leapt from the cab, arms flailing, shouting absolutely clear Anglo-Saxon obscenities in our wake. Suddenly the traffic started moving again, and only another bus bearing down on his rear bumper persuaded the taxi driver to resume his place behind the wheel.

The sun had gone behind the clouds; I turned my coat

collar up. Too Tall Tom held on to my elbow, adjusting his long strides to my short ones.

I began. "Okay, what the hell is going on with Modesty?"

"Well—er—in regard to . . ." He stammered.

"In regard to Rickie Romero, that's what!" I yelled. Too Tall Tom tightened his grip on my arm. "For starters, did the cat burglar present Modesty with the chunk of Fort Knox that's dangling from the chain around her neck? I hope she realizes that carrying all that weight will give her a dowager's hump."

"Jake, please . . . I'm not supposed to say any—"

"If Rickie's her houseguest, our fellow ghost is guilty of aiding and abetting. Talk to me! Where did she meet him? And how did their 'relationship' bloom so damn fast?"

"Okay." Too Tall Tom sighed. "I hate to violate a confidence, but I'm just as frantic as you are about Modesty's behavior. So out of character. We have to do something, don't we?"

I brought my left hand across my chest and squeezed his fingers, which were wrapped around my right elbow. "We do."

"Actually, they only ran into each other yesterday morning while the mechanics finished working on—what turned out to be—their identical Volkswagens. Same year. Same color. *Quelle bonne chance, n'est-ce pas?* Anyway, there they were, waiting together, at that garage Modesty uses. Over on Eleventh Avenue. Rickie invited her for a cup of coffee to pass the time. Then, darling, the thunderbolt." Too Tall Tom twirled me around him. "Like Al Pacino as Michael in *The Godfather*! Not with Diane Keaton. With that girl he married in Sicily. She died; later he married Diane. Or like me, with that warlock last year. One look and it's love."

We did a little hip-hopping two-step, then he spun me under his arm. I realized we were swing dancing down the block. "Haven't you ever been struck by the thunderbolt, Jake?"

Though I hated to admit it—even to myself—I hadn't. Unless I could count that quarter-of-a-century-old bite that I'd taken out of Dennis. That encounter had shaken me up. And its aftershock still lingered.

I didn't answer his question, asking one instead. "When this is all over, will you teach me the Lindy hop?"

Too Tall Tom promised, seemingly grateful that I had changed the subject. However, I hadn't. Expressing my desire to swing had been an aside. I said, "So what happened after she was hit by this thunderbolt? And by the way, was it mutual? I mean, were they struck simultaneously?"

"That is always the question, isn't it, darling? Modesty certainly thinks so. Romero came calling late last night, just showed up on her doorstep—"

"And she let him in?"

"Modesty wanted to believe him. She's mad about the boy, Jake! Thunderstruck! It's clear you've never been!" Too Tall Tom sounded sorry for me. "Rickie arrived, proclaiming his innocence, swearing he'd been set up and bearing his gift . . . a cross of gold. And—um— well, I gather they didn't play chess all night."

"Jesus! Is he still there?"

"Rickie was sound asleep when she left to meet me this morning. But he could be gone by now."

"Do you realize that we're on Modesty's street? Is this fate or what?" I felt we were about to to get some answers. "Her apartment house is just off Lexington.

Would you believe I've never been there? Have you?"

"Once, when we were both attending that dysfunctional-chakra class. My second chakra had shut down completely, and I was worried sick that it would never open up again. I remember stopping there for a nice cup of tea." Hmmphf! Turning to Modesty for tea and sympathy! Whose best friend was he, anyway?

Watching me, Too Tall Tom ceased his reminiscences and said, "Don't get any bright ideas, Jake. We are not going to Modesty's apartment. Rickie promised her that he would be moving on today, though I think that will break her heart."

I had a hard time casting Modesty as a romantic heroine. Risking everything to save the man she loved. "Yeah, well, Modesty may take Rickie at his word, but I don't. Why don't you go to the wake and I'll catch up with you?"

We were crossing Park Avenue—or trying to—many of these drivers also ignored red lights. Too Tall Tom forged a path through the traffic to the safety of the divide. After we navigated, from there, to the other side of the avenue, Modesty's building would be three-quarters of a block dead ahead. I waited, impatiently, for the light to change to green and Too Tall Tom to change his mind.

We were almost under Modesty's building's canopy, however, before he spoke. "Damn it, Jake! I can't allow you to do this alone. I want to protect Modesty, too. But should we call Ben and tell him about Rickie? Oh God! Do we dare allow the police to deal with this? What do you say?"

"I say let's see if he's there first! Then we can make our decision!"

Too Tall Tom was still wrestling with his conscience

when the doorman opened the door and Hunter Green dashed out of Modesty's lobby and made a quick left toward Lexington. I don't think he noticed Too Tall Tom and me staring at him in horror.

Twenty-four

"Ben Rubin could be right!" I choked, feeling shaky and disloyal, then continued, "It looks like Hunter Green and Rickie Romero are in this together!"

"I'm going to follow Hunter!" Too Tall Tom's long legs were moving east. "You call Ben, when he arrives, you can check out Rickie!" As he sped around the corner on Lexington, his last words, shouted over his shoulder and almost lost in the wind, were, "Wait for the police; don't you dare go up there alone!"

I tried all three of Ben's numbers, leaving the same message: Urgent! Call me! But not saying why. I guess, if still possible, I wanted to protect Modesty. Then I paced from canopy to corner and back again, eliciting puzzled glances from the doorman. This was not an ethical question. I hadn't promised Too Tall Tom anything. And God knows when I'd hear from Ben. Of course, I could call 911. Or I could buzz up to the apartment. Though Rickie Romero probably wouldn't answer the buzzer. Too dangerous. He could be gone by now, though not via the front door. He could be dead. Killed by Hunter. Jesus, how could I even think such trash? Now, if there were only some way I could sneak into the building. I'd just knock on Modesty's door and see if Rickie answered. How could I get by that sourpuss doorman? He acted as if he were St. Peter, guarding the portals to heaven, and I were Lucifer, trying to worm my way back in.

An elegant old lady's runaway dog gave me an opportunity to gate-crash. While I loitered near the door, St. Peter held it open, as a contemporary version of the Duchess of Windsor, carrying not a pug but a poodle, strolled out. The dog suddenly leapt from her arm and took off into the traffic. Horns blared and tires screeched as drivers swerved, trying to avoid hitting the animal. The lady screamed, "Save my Lancelot!" With the poodle's weeping mistress close behind, the doorman hastened to retrieve the yelping pooch, abandoning his post . . . and allowing the door slowly to swing shut. But before that could happen, I grabbed it and ducked inside the lobby. The concierge looked up from his racing form, completely unaware of all the commotion, and smiled at me. "Yes, madam. How may I help you?"

I entered the elevator, glad to be on my way up to 1313, before the doorman discovered I'd disappeared. Since most New York City buildings don't have a thirteenth floor, I decided that Modesty must have searched long and hard for this particular apartment.

Standing in the hallway, afraid to knock, I felt like the wife in *The Shining,* about to be scared to death by what lurked behind the door. Timidly, I raised my hand, made a fist, and tapped. Gently. Unless Rickie had been standing there listening, he'd never hear me. Moments passed. No response. My throat felt dry. And my hand, as I rapped again—louder this time—shook. God! What if Rickie really was dead? Then I thought I heard something and leaned in closer. A voice whispered, "Modesty?"

"Yes," I said. Then waited. The peephole cover slid to one side and a dark brown eye peered out. "You'd better let me in, the police are on their way!" I marveled at my smooth delivery of such a bold-faced lie.

The door opened and Rickie Romero, dressed in his usual black, stood there smiling, exposing all those great teeth, as if he were glad to see me. "Come in, *cara*." Said the spider to the fly. "What a pleasant surprise. I thought you were attending Senator Fione's wake with Modesty."

As Rickie locked the door behind us, I asked myself: Why wasn't I?

The charm of the apartment took my mind off murder. Wow! Who'd have thought that Modesty's home would remind me of a cottage in Victorian England? With touches of Martha Stewart. Or maybe they were Too Tall Tom's touches. Or, maybe, Modesty had a happy heart . . . however well hidden. The living room was wonderful. Velvet and silk. Crystal vases holding fresh flowers, and quaint, elegant furnishings: overstuffed, claret-colored, cut-velvet armchairs, a whimsical, antique chandler painted in white enamel, and a camelback couch in a claret-and-white silk print. At the far end of the long, narrow room, a floor-to-ceiling, uncovered glass door led to a tiny balcony filled with plants.

"Why are you here, Jake?" Rickie's soft voice startled me.

"The question is: Why are you here, Rickie? How dare you compromise my friend?" I ignored his snicker. "You'll cause Modesty tons of trouble. The police will be here any minute! Ben Rubin knows I'm with you and he thinks you killed Carita." As the words tumbled out, I regretted turning off my phone, putting myself in yet another dumb and dangerous position.

"And what do you think, Jake?" He still spoke in that low, soothing, sexual tone, but his lithe body had tensed. "Do you believe that I poisoned Holly Halligan and the senator? Then killed Carita? That I'm taking advantage of Modesty?"

Was he guilty of the murders? With all those other suspects, how could I be certain? I was certain about one thing. "Whether you killed them or not, you've put Modesty in jeopardy! And what the hell was Hunter Green doing here?"

"Unlike your unexpected visit, I'd invited Hunter. There was something I needed to tell him. In person."

"About the Faith diamond!" I said. "You've changed its hiding place, haven't you?"

Rickie looked startled for a second, then grinned. "You're one super sleuth, Jake. With that creative a mind, you should give up ghosting and start pedaling your own fiction."

"I know I'm right. Hunter thought he had access to the Faith, but you've changed the venue, haven't you? Ben Rubin thinks you and Hunter are partners—"

"Let me assure you, I work alone, Jake." Rickie moved closer to me. "You really didn't call the police, did you?" I backed away, stumbling. A loud rap on the door brought us both to a halt.

"This is the doorman!" an angry voice from the hall shouted. "Open up, young lady, I know you're in there!"

Rickie extended his right arm and reached for mine. I screamed.

"Sorry to rush off like this, Jake! But I must be on

my way." Bowing, he lifted my hand to his lips and kissed it. Then he spun his tight body full circle, strode across the room, and opened the sliding-glass that led to the balcony. "Ciao, *cara.* There are two things you must believe: I've murdered no one and I love Modesty. Deeply, madly, truly! Please tell her to hold that thought close to her heart until I return!" He waved, stepped out onto the balcony, vaulted over the railing, and was gone. I ran to see where, but by the time I reached the railing, the cat burglar had vanished.

Twenty-five

Police barricades helped contain the several-blocks-long line waiting to view the senator's body. Two hours late and totally unnerved, I went to the front of the queue, praying that Mom's information had been accurate and I would find my name among those on the "invited mourners" list. A Campbell's employee, dressed in a morning jacket with tails, an ascot, and gray striped trousers, together with a Secret Service type macho guy wearing a black suit, white shirt, and sunglasses, stood at the door, checking off names. Before I could give them mine, I heard Too Tall Tom shout, "Hey, Jake!"

I walked back to where he and Jane were standing, none too close to the entrance. "It seems only the politicians, the Crime Writers, the Teamsters Union, the senator's family, his closest friends—and your mother—are on that damn list," Jane said. "Maura and Modesty waltzed right on in, then so did Gypsy Rose, almost an hour ago, but I've been on this bloody line since two! And Too Tall Tom would have been relegated to waiting over on the FDR Drive if I hadn't spotted him and made him hop over the barricade."

"Pushy, that's what I call it!" Mrs. McMahon, her handbag shoved into Jane's back, said. "Your fancy friend here has some nerve, letting that giant in ahead of those who stand and wait. Don't think you're going to squeeze in front of me, too, Jake O'Hara!"

Damn! How could I ask Too Tall Tom about Hunter with this old biddy hanging on my every word?

"Go on ahead, Jake," Too Tall Tom told me. "Hunter Green's inside. Jane and I will talk to you later."

"Thanks!" I turned to my nosy neighbor, noticing that her daughter was nowhere in sight. Patricia Ann, the Mary Kay company's rising star, must have taken off in her pink Cadillac. "Sorry if my friends inconvenienced you, Mrs. McMahon; they were following my orders." Wasn't I too bitchy? But loving the role! "And don't worry, I won't be needing a place on line, I have an invitation."

It took several angst-filled moments for the door patrol to find my name. I figured that God had punished me . . . my brassy retort had backfired . . . reinforcing the fact that a ghost has no identity. Wouldn't I look lame if my name didn't show up on that list? Finally, I walked through the specially-installed-for-the-senator's-viewing metal detector and into Campbell's carefully calculated serenity.

Edwina Carrington Fione, her cool composure seemingly every bit as calculated, stood next to the junior senator from New York. The widow, as always, elegantly tailored and coiffed, shook hands and offered a greeting to everyone who entered. I found myself surrounded by interesting companions: Mercury Rising, the rock star, pranced in front of me and Wanda Sparks slunk close behind me.

"Jake, I have to talk to you, now!" Wanda whispered as I watched Mercury Rising kiss Mrs. Fione on both cheeks, then extend his gloved hand to the junior senator. I wondered how the heavy-metal star and the Washington socialite had crossed paths. Old Edwina appeared to have eclectic friendships.

A jab in my lower back was followed by another breathless request. "Where can we be alone? I know. Meet me in the ladies' room!" Wanda Sparks's choice of meeting place was, to say the least, intriguing. While she ranked high on my list of suspects, I really needed to speak to Hunter Green, who topped her.

She'd have to wait her turn. "In ten minutes," I said over my shoulder as I approached Edwina. Wanda groaned in my left ear, but I ignored her and smiled at the widow Fione. "I'm so sorry—"

"Yes, my dear, I'm sure you are. All of New York is sorry. But I'd like you to find Gypsy Rose Liebowitz and ask her to join me here. Immediately. Thanks so much. Oh, forgive me, Miss O'Hara, please allow me to introduce you to our state's one remaining senator . . ."

Wanda poked me again. This time her whisper could be heard in the world beyond. "Now, Jake. It's a matter of life and—"

The senator smiled graciously, then dismissed me, preparing to face Wanda, whom Edwinda Fione was greeting with great warmth.

"Jake!" The funeral home's reception area, filled with so many bodies, no doubt violating every city fire ordinance on the book, made it difficult for me to locate Dennis. "Over here, to your right," he called. "Near the chapel."

I forged through the crowd, anxious to reach him. As always, his voice had sent a shiver through my system . . . down to my toes. A lifelong thunderbolt?

Unfortunately, Wendy Wu, ANN's anchor and Dennis Kim's ex-wife, had left her desk to mourn with the masses and, sexy in a short skirt and trendy heels, was standing at his side. Dennis's gold-flecked eyes cast a concerned look at me. "Where have you been, Jake? Your mother's worried. We all were."

Wendy Wu's gaze showed no charity. "Why, hello, Jake. It's been years. Isn't it amazing that you still remind me so much of Annie Hall? How nice to see that some people never bother to change with the current times . . . or fashions."

Dennis brushed off his ex as if she were a virus-carrying mosquito and led me through the line of mourners, who were, slowly, passing by the bier then returning to the foyer. Senator Fione's body had been laid out in an ornate mahogany casket. Tall lighted candles stood like sentinels, guarding his head and feet. Wreaths and baskets of flowers, mostly gladiolas, which I hate, were crowded into the chapel and their sweet, sickly scent filled the room. A lady circling the corpse said, "Doesn't he look grand?"

A heavyset man agreed. "Never better!" I wondered, would that box be burned with the body? Campbell's couldn't recycle a casket, could they? A hell of a lot of money might go up in smoke when Charlie Fione was cremated.

Mom sat in the last row of the chapel, wiping away a tear. Since my mother cried at *Hallmark Hall of Fame* shows' commercials, I would have been a bit disappointed if my brief vanishing act had left her dry-eyed. She greeted me with, "I tried to call; why do you carry a cell phone if you're not going to answer it?"

Gypsy Rose, dressed in gray cashmere and a matching fedora, sat next to Mom and joined in the guilt chorus. "There's a killer on the loose, Jake! And we had no way of knowing what happened to you."

Feeling as bad as they'd intended that I should, I said, "I had an unexpected meeting and I shut the phone off. Look, I'm really sorry." My mother seemed somewhat mollified, crumpling her tissue and patting my hand, so I quickly changed the subject. "Gypsy Rose, Edwina Fione says that she has to speak to you immediately."

"What kind of meeting?" my mother asked as Gypsy Rose headed for the foyer.

"Mom, let's talk about that at home." I scanned the room. "Where's Modesty?"

Dennis laughed. "Modesty *did* receive a phone call. About ten or fifteen minutes ago. From a man." He twirled an invisible mustache, leering at me like Groucho Marx. "We haven't seen her since, but we presume that she left for a rendezvous with her mystery man."

"She's stranger than ever, Jake!" my mother said. "And where did she get that gold cross? Modesty wouldn't tell me, but it's as big as one of the treasures from the Vatican's vault. What is going on? Could it be love?"

Now guilt galloped like the Four Horsemen, with Death racing through my veins. "Stay put, Mom, I'll be back." I turned to Dennis. "Please, help me find Hunter. Now!" My voice cracked. "I, er . . . have you seen him? I need—"

Dennis took my arm, but addressed my mother. "Maura, please don't worry; I promise I won't leave Jake's side." Then he said to me, "I saw Hunter in the lounge a while back. Come on, let's go get him."

We'd made it halfway across the chapel, taking advantage of small gaps in the never-ending line, to inch our way toward the foyer, when Wanda blocked our path. "Jake!" she shrieked. "What kind of a charter member of Ghostwriters Anonymous are you? How can you refuse to come to the aid of a sister ghost?" Gotcha! She had me.

"Okay, Wanda, just give me a second here!" I pulled Dennis away from her earshot and said, "Listen, I think Modesty is with Rickie Romero—she's been hiding him at her house—and I have reason to believe that Hunter may be working with Rickie. Or was. Anyway, track Hunter down, and don't let him out of your sight. Too Tall Tom should be inside any minute now, he can update you on Hunter and Rickie. Jesus, I've made some major mistakes! Call Ben; he may be trying to reach me. Let him know that Modesty's in danger, but don't say that Rickie stayed overnight with her!" I sighed. "And I guess you'd better tell him about Hunter, too. I'm going to the ladies' room with Wanda."

Dennis stared at me, then shook his head. "Damn it, Jake! I promised your mother that I'd stay with you. Do not, I repeat, do *not* leave this funeral parlor. Is that understood?"

In the powder room, Wanda walked straight to the mirror and began to brush the teased tower out of her dark hair. It looked like torture. While starting the reconstruction process, she said, "Rickie's going to kill me next." Watching those frenzied fingers still tugging at her hair, I heard the terror in her voice.

The door opened and Gypsy Rose came in. "Hi, Wanda, aiming for new heights? Jake, the mayor's with Edwina, and her brother-in-law, you know, the pastor of Sacred Heart, just arrived to say the rosary, so she can't talk now. I'm going over to her house tonight, and I'd like you to come with me."

I sensed that Gypsy Rose didn't want to give any more details in front of Wanda. "Okay. Just let me know when. And please tell Mom that I'll be back in the chapel before the final decade."

But would I return in time for the last sorrowful mystery? Wanda's fear fed my own. She believed that Rickie had killed three people and would kill again. And I believed that wherever Rickie had gone, he'd taken Modesty with him.

"Does this have something to do with your robbery?" I asked.

"Yes, I'm sure Rickie robbed me." Wanda pulled a long thin comb through strands that looked tired. "After all, that *is* his profession, isn't it? And the notes that were stolen pointed clearly to his guilt! Jake, I can't find Modesty and I want to do a mini fourth step right now!"

I knew that damn robbery had been important. Why, in God's name, hadn't I followed up on it sooner? "Wanda, what did those papers reveal?"

"His dirty laundry. All the steamy stuff about Hell's Kitchen that he'd left out of *Cat on Trump Tower's Roof.*"

"Tell me!"

"One hot summer, more than fifty years ago, a fourteen-year-old boy raped a beautiful young woman." Frightened or not, Wanda obviously relished this opportunity to show off her storytelling ability to a rapt audience of one. "Helen Mary Houlihan had been spending the summer with her cousins in Hell's Kitchen while working as a maid over on Park Avenue. After the rape, she never went home again. Back in Plattsburgh, Rickie Romero's grandmother's kid brother, an immigrant who'd fallen in love with Helen Mary, committed suicide after receiving a 'Dear Caesar' letter, following her disappearance. For three generations, the Romero family has vowed revenge on the unknown rapist who ruined two lives. When Grannie, calling from her deathbed, reached Rickie in prison, he hired a private detective to find Helen Mary Houlihan. Of course, her life hadn't been ruined—she'd emerged as Holly Halligan. Finally, old—and bold—enough to confront her ugly past, which MGM's publicity department had expunged, Holly met with Rickie and revealed the rapist's name."

"Charlie Fione!"

"How did you know that? You spoiled the O. Henry ending!"

"Wanda, listen to me. As a member of Ghostwriters Anonymous, you have to tell me the truth. Were you the leprechaun? Did you, however innocently, help Rickie Romero to poison the panel?"

"I swear, Jake, I didn't! I've given that a lot of thought. Rickie has a huge, if weird, fawning fan club; he'd have had no problem finding someone to play that part."

"Have you told Ben Rubin all this?"

"No, but I can't keep any more secrets. I'm telling him this afternoon." She checked her watch. "According to the information that homicide gave me, he should be here any minute."

Jesus, I thought, Rickie not only had inherited Holly Halligan's fortune, but, with the senator's murder, Great-Uncle Caesar's honor had been avenged! And now Romero himself had vanished, along with Modesty!

Twenty-six

I sat in a stall, curled into a fetal position, on top of the closed toilet seat. Arms wrapped around legs, which I'd pulled up to my chest, with my head abutting my knees. I was hiding out, trying to fight off tears of frustration. God! What a mess! And I had no one to blame but myself. If I'd only waited for Ben to call, Rickie would be in jail and Modesty would be safe. Yet even as I decided that Romero had to be the killer, somewhere, in the tiny recording studio located in the far recesses of my mind, a tape of Rickie's last words before he'd leapt from the balcony kept replaying: "I've murdered no one and I love Modesty. Deeply, madly, truly!"

With the evidence that Wanda had hand-delivered, Rickie's black lines, leading to double motives, would spread across Jane's chart, affirming his guilt, so why couldn't I erase the memory of that look of love on Rickie's face or turn off the tape?

"Deeply, madly, truly! Tell her to hold that thought close to her heart," he'd said. If Rickie had been planning on phoning Modesty at Campbell's, he damn knew he could tell her that himself. Then, maybe, he hadn't thought that far ahead, calling her on the spur of the moment. Or, maybe, Rickie hadn't been the one who called!

"You're a bitch! A bleached-blond bitch!" My musings had been rudely interrupted. Startled, I almost fell off the john. "A low-down, lying, gold-digging, sick slut, that's what you are, Ashley Butler!" Venus DeMill slurred her insults. But what was lost in clarity was more than made up for in volume. "I'm going to pull your Southern Fried hair out by its black roots."

"Shut up, Venus, you're drunk and you're crazy!" Ashley's accent had lost any semblance of its sweet-as-syrup sound. Much more like Tallulah's Regina than Vivien's Scarlett.

"Don't you call me crazy! How dare you parade around town, with that mile-high mall hair and obscene miniskirt, telling other writers that you were the great Carita Magenta's ghost? Why are you doing this? And here Carita is dead." Venus broke into sobs. "Not able to defend herself. Well, I won't let you get away with this crap. You couldn't hold a crayon to Carita's colorful style. Her distinctive voice. Her New York edge. You trailer-trash tramp. Do you think anyone will believe your dirty, rotten lies?"

"Well now, maybe you didn't know Carita as well as you thought you did, Venus!" Ashley hissed.

"I'll kill you, you piece of Mississippi mud! I'll tear that lying tongue out of your filthy mouth!"

A sudden lilt of laughter—Ashley's—unnerved me almost as much as the verbal abuse that the two women had been heaping on each other. "It's Georgia, darling. Peach Street in Atlanta. Not far from where Miss Pittypat lived. And I think you should know that Maurice Welch believes me." Some of the sap again dripped from Ashley Butler's voice. "I think the poor, dear old lush is worried that you killed your lover. I might have blamed his ramblings on a wet brain, but since you've been threatening my life, I've reconsidered. Maybe one drunk can identify with a fellow drunk's motive. So tell me, Venus, did you do it? Or do you think Maurice murdered Carita Magenta in order to protect his vested interest in you?"

Venus roared like a wounded animal. Then I heard a loud slap, followed by a scream and a crash. The door to my stall flew open and Ashley came charging in, like a projectile, knocking me off the toilet seat.

She made a quick recovery, regaining her balance and rubbing her raw cheek. "Thank God you're so soft, Jake. I could have landed on the porcelain and really hurt myself."

"Ashley, you should have ended up in the toilet bowl, where a turd like you belongs!" Venus said, then reached into the stall and helped me to stand.

"Jake, a lady always makes her presence known," Ashley said. "We had no notion that you were squirreled away in a stall, eavesdropping on our private conversation."

"Shut up, trailer trash!" Venus pulled a flask from her bag and took a large swig. "The damage is done. Jake, in my judgment, you're smart enough not to repeat the rantings of a crazed bitch. Is that a correct conclusion?" The last word was slurred almost beyond comprehension. She wiped off the flask and passed it to me.

I gulped down some brown liquid and gagged. Scotch. I've always hated the taste of scotch. "Correct!" I choked out. Venus DeMill was one big broad; I didn't want to be flung into a stall.

"Yes, sugar." Ashley Butler's antebellum belle was back in full bloom. "And I'm confident that you also will conclude that poor Venus is a lifetime lush and her accusations, which, incidentally, border on libel, have no merit. As a good ghost, I can say no more."

I handed the flask back to Venus, brushed torn sheets of discarded toilet paper and other bits of disgusting debris from my pantsuit, feeling grateful that I hadn't worn the DKNY number that my mother had been pushing, and—well trained by Mom—scrubbed my hands and face, then applied lipstick and blush.

"You could use some more color, Jake," Ashley gushed. "You're pale as a . . . well . . . you know what."

Before either Venus or I could kill her, the door opened and the one remaining senator from New York joined us. I left her with two of her craziest constituents.

I don't remember Times Square at midnight on Y2K being any more crowded than Campbell's lounge was this afternoon. Ben and I had celebrated the last night of the last year of the twentieth century together. A corny, old-fashioned romantic date. We attended the Christmas show at Radio City Music Hall, had dinner at the Algonquin, and walked over to Forty-second Street hand in hand to watch the ball fall. Now, with the way I'd screwed up his investigation, he'd probably never speak to me again.

Hunter Green. I had to talk to him! Among other things, he might know where Rickie had gone. Had Dennis found Hunter? And how would I find Dennis?

Suddenly shoved too close to the public wall phone, I spied Donald Jay's narrow lips moving a mile a millisecond as he shouted into the speaker, trying to be heard above the chatter of the crowd. Engrossed in his own monologue, he didn't see me. Blocked for the moment by two large bodies, I wasn't going anywhere. So, as Ashley had accused me of doing earlier, I shamelessly eavesdropped.

"Who knew the bastard would be dead in a couple of months?" Donald laughed. "Yeah. Well, I think she's in our pocket now. Since the vote has been delayed . . ."

The larger of the two bodies inched forward. I shadowed him, away from the wall. I'd almost made it, without being spotted, going behind Donald's back, heading into the slow-moving mass of humanity, when my cell phone rang. Jay jerked around and glared at me. "This is a funeral home, Ms. O'Hara; your blaring phone is disturbing the mourners!"

"And you're killing the environment!" I said, then immediately rued my big mouth, even before he slammed down his phone, pulled mine out of my hand, and threw it to the floor.

One of the big guys squatted and retrieved my still-ringing phone while the other pushed Donald Jay down on his knees, ordering him to "tell the lady you're sorry."

This had to be the liveliest wake in Campbell's history!

"Hello . . . hello . . ." I said, retracing my steps to the ladies' room, where I might or might not have some privacy. Lots of static. Probably a result of Donald Jay tossing my phone around like a football. "Hello . . ." I pushed open the door of the ladies' room.

"Jake, this is Hunter."

"Where are you? I need to talk to you!"

"Interesting. I need to talk to you, too. Meet me at my house in a half hour. With all the traffic at this hour, you'd better take the train. And Jake, what I have to say is completely confidential; come alone." He hung up.

The senator and Mrs. McMahon were engaged in a debate about eye shadow: the former pro earth tones; the latter in favor of matching your shadow to your outfit. I backed out the door.

There was no way I could duck out of here without giving an itinerary to Mom, Gypsy Rose, and Dennis. Too Tall Tom and Jane, too. If they'd arrived inside and if I could find them. There wasn't much time: Tribeca would be a long haul, even on the subway.

Dealing with Mom wouldn't be easy. She'd carry on about detecting being dangerous, then pull out all the stops, including using Gypsy Rose's and Dennis's considerable powers of persuasion. As I debated what to do—with my baser instincts winning—I spotted Too Tall Tom, standing head and shoulders above the crowd. "Yo," I yelled, totally ignoring the sensibilities of my fellow mourners.

Taking giant steps, Too Tall Tom arrived at my side in seconds.

"Where's Jane?" I asked.

"Looking for the ladies' room."

I laughed. "Campbell's hot spot."

"You do realize that we were waiting a long time," Too Tall Tom said, "and it was damn cold out there! Did you find Hunter?"

"He must have slipped out. But I've just spoken to him on the phone; I'm on my way to his loft now."

"Well, you're not going alone, Jake, I'll come with you!"

Damn! How could I get rid of him? Maybe . . . a plot began to percolate. "Listen, I want you to explain things to Mom first. Tell her that I had to leave; fudge about why. Then follow me to Hunter's. Oh! Ask Dennis if he reached Ben. Wanda said he was on his way here. Modesty's among the missing! I didn't want Ben to know that she'd hidden Rickie, but I'm afraid she's taken off with him again."

If Too Tall Tom talked to my mother and Dennis while they were interrogating him, I'd have at least a twenty-minute head start. Plenty of time for me to get some answers from Hunter and to honor the spirit, if not the actual letter, of his request that I come alone. Though feeling disloyal to Hunter, I decided that it might be a smart move to have Too Tall Tom as backup. God knows, I hadn't made too many smart moves today.

I made one now, dashing for the door before he had a chance to say no.

Twenty-seven

Hunter looked like hell. Much the way I felt. Hanging on to a pole, in a packed-like-sardines subway car, all the way from the Upper East Side to lower Manhattan would have turned Mother Teresa into a card-carrying capitalist. Fantasy Island—the New York built on dreams, Woody Allen movies, and my mother's memories—crumbled like sand castles and smelled like Secaucus when one was traveling downtown during rush hour. I'd clutched my bag to my bosom, closed my eyes, and pictured myself being transported in Dennis Kim's cream-colored Rolls-Royce.

During my journey, it had grown dark. With no sun streaming through the loft's cathedral ceiling's skylight, the glow had gone. The huge room, like Hunter, seemed to have lost its luster.

"A drink, Jake?" He motioned with the glass he held in his right hand; I suspected it wasn't his first. "This is scotch, but I can offer you most anything."

"No, thank you." I sank into the same crushed velvet

Art Deco chair that I'd sat in during my first visit. "Look, Hunter, a lot of really strange stuff has been happening. We have to talk . . . you know . . . to straighten some things out."

Hunter, too, again opted for the matching love seat, facing me. "Strange stuff. Well put, Jake. Would you like to elaborate?"

I shoved my bangs out of my eyes. Something was very wrong. While I'd been feeling uncomfortable up to then, I now felt fear. This is mad. I'm sitting across from a Pulitzer Prize–winning author, my personal hero, and a well-respected member of the community, almost convinced that he might be a multiple murderer. Ben had said that Hunter couldn't have killed Carita. Indeed, Ben and his partner, Cassidy, were his alibi. However, if Rickie had drowned Carita, and Hunter and he were in this together . . .

"You thinking that I may have murdered Holly and the senator, aren't you, Jake?"

My fingers dug into the crushed-velvet arms of the club chair. I could find no words.

"I didn't." Hunter leaned forward and met my eyes. "Though I can understand how you—and the police— could have concluded that I'm guilty. And the reasons for those conclusions are, for the most part, my fault. You spotted me leaving Modesty's this afternoon, didn't you?"

"How did you know?" I stammered.

"Too Tall Tom's too big to be a successful tail, Jake." Hunter smiled. "I led him to Campbell's, knowing I'd be allowed in but he'd have to wait on line. I hung around long enough for a few people to see me, then I ducked out the basement door. The one the dead bodies are carried through. That's quite a setup they have down there. As a murder-mystery ghost, you should visit it sometime."

"Why were you at Modesty's?" I finally found my voice. Curiosity conquering fright. And I wanted, so much, to believe him.

"Let's backtrack for a moment." Hunter sipped his scotch. "I was convinced that Rickie Romero had murdered Carita Magenta. He certainly had motive, means, and opportunity . . . in fact, he was seen leaving the scene of the crime. And Jake, that's where he'd stashed the Faith diamond. When I heard about the drowning, I assumed Rickie had returned to retrieve the jewel. And killed Carita to keep her quiet. That's about the only way any man could shut that woman up."

"Whoa!" I said. "How did you know that Carita had the diamond?"

"When Wanda was—um—editing for Rickie, she discovered that the night Romero robbed Magenta, a strong bond had formed between the cat and Carita. The chapter, covering the robbery that segued into a wild party, became a nightmare for Wanda. Rickie seemed torn between truth and consequence . . . under no circumstances did he want to upset Carita. Wanda claimed that Rickie tried to be as vague as possible regarding the identities of the ladies in question, but Carita was furious. And though Rickie insisted to all and sundry that the chapter, like the book, was all fiction, Carita wanted revenge.

"Are you saying that the bond between Rickie and Carita was the Faith diamond?"

"Smart lady. Exactly! After downing too many cocktails and swapping too many confidences, Rickie conned Carita into keeping the stone for him. For a price, of course. A sort of room-and-board arrangement."

"What about Venus?" I asked, thinking about her

heavy drinking and her total lack of discretion. "Didn't she know that Carita had the stone?"

Hunter smiled again. "No, my dear, Venus had passed out long before Rickie and Carita negotiated the future hiding place of the Faith diamond."

"Why in God's name would Wanda have told you all this? It makes no sense. She thinks Rickie's the killer, too. She's frightened to death of him . . . at least that's what she told me this afternoon at the senator's wake."

"You must remember there had been no murders when she first discussed these matters with me. And that I arranged for Wanda's assignment with Rickie. She considered me her mentor. A father figure. Anything that she told me she knew I would keep in complete confidence. Actually, while chatting with Romero in his cell and listening to his recounting of the robberies he'd gotten away with, I already suspected that Carita Magenta had provided the Faith diamond with a safe house." Hunter rose, walked to the bar, refilled his scotch, and turned to me. "Are you sure you won't join me?"

I sighed. "A small white wine, please." I stood at the bar while he rummaged on the shelves for the Chablis, the ice bucket, and a proper glass. "And Rickie Romero has been aware for some time that you figured out where the Faith diamond was stashed, hasn't he, Hunter? As you yourself once told me, knowing the diamond's location gave you a major motive for killing Rickie. Is that why you went to Modesty's apartment today?"

Hunter handed me the glass of wine. "Do you really believe that I went there to kill him?" He chuckled. "If truth be told, I was so angry, so full of vengeance, I could have killed Rickie. But I'd gone there, totally irrational, I might add, to accuse him of murder and to see if there wasn't some way I could get my hands on the diamond before the police arrested him." He sat down again, picked up his drink, then said, "Greed is an ugly thing. I'd lost Angela. And I'd lost a small fortune to Ashes Away. Dr. Nujurian was ready to turn me in to Ben Rubin, for sending her those threatening letters. The police had searched my home, accused me of murder, humiliated me. Then Rickie took back the Faith. Before I'd had the chance. I confess I wanted that diamond."

"How did you know that Rickie was staying at Modesty's apartment?" I sat, sipping my wine, trying to buy time to think. I wasn't sure how much, if any, of Hunter's tale I found credible. I would have expected a true-crime writer of his caliber to develop a far better plotline than this.

"The bastard called me to brag! And to taunt me. While Rickie was in that cell, I guess he never heard about caller ID."

"So you hit star sixty-nine and Modesty Meade's name showed up."

"Yes. Then, in a rage, I went up there."

"Had Rickie boasted that he drown Carita as well?" This story sucked.

"No, just that he'd reclaimed the diamond. Rickie told me that Magenta had taped it under one of the legs on her purple tub. He laughed, saying how he kept picturing Venus taking all those bubble baths, never realizing that there she was sitting naked on top of a fortune. Of course, at the time I thought he killed Carita."

"At the time?" I asked. "You mean you don't think so now?" Was this another of Hunter's plot twists or what?

"When Rickie arrived at Carita's, she was already dead. Her head in the bathtub and a plate of lasagna on the kitchen table. Romero knew he'd be the numero uno suspect, so he removed the diamond and himself from the premises; however, a neighbor witnessed his hasty departure.

"That's what Rickie told you?" I wondered if Hunter had totally lost it—or thought I had. "And you believed him?"

"Jake, I've researched and written about the criminal mind for longer than you've been alive." Hunter sounded patronizing. I questioned why I'd ever regarded him as my hero. "Naturally, I wouldn't take a man like Romero at his word. I look for logic before making a final judgment; the rest of his story provided me with one certainty: Rickie Romero had no rational reason for murdering either Holly Halligan or Senator Fione. Since the person who'd poisoned them also killed Carita, it follows that it couldn't be Rickie."

"What the hell are you talking about?" I jumped out of my chair. "With Holly's death, Rickie inherited her empire and Charlie Fione's murder avenged the Romero family's honor. How can you say Rickie had no motives?"

"Logic, Jake. Logic, the great clarifier, indicates that the cat is in the clear. Look, with the Faith diamond waiting under Carita's tub, Rickie didn't need Holly's money—and he knew that, eventually, he'd have it all. Furthermore, he really liked her. Under other circumstances, she would have been his great-aunt. Why would he kill her?" Hunter finished his drink. "And Holly Halligan had told Rickie about Edwina arranging Charlie Fione's Ashes Away cruise and his appointment with Dr. Nujurian. So Rickie knew that the senator had a very short time to live. Why kill a dead man? Rickie had served his time. He hated prison. Now, as a rich man, he wanted to live his life to the hilt. Aware of the senator's doomed destiny, why would Rickie put all his dreams in jeopardy?"

I'd had my own doubts about Rickie's guilt, but had been afraid my judgment was colored by feelings not fact. Now Hunter's twisted tale reinforced those doubts. "But . . . if Rickie isn't the killer, where is he? And whodunit?"

"Those are the questions we have to answer, Jake!" Modesty said, walking out of the shadows.

Twenty-eight

Trying not to sound like my mother, I explained to Modesty that we'd all been worried about her and that Too Tall Tom would be arriving any minute. Her affect wandered between quiet desperation and barely repressed anger. The latter directed at me. Had she spoken to Rickie? Or had she tried to reach him and failed, assuming that he'd flown from her nest? Did she know that I'd paid an uninvited visit to her apartment, nosed around in her private life, and incited her one and only boyfriend to jump off the balcony? Hunter had seen me lurking under her canopy with Too Tall Tom. And since he, not Rickie, had phoned Modesty at Campbell's, no doubt he'd shared that tidbit with her.

I finished my wine, then, too late, remembered my mother's warning to watch what I drank, lest it be laced with cyanide. Oh well, if Hunter had poisoned me, Modesty would be an eyewitness and could testify at his trial. A few moments passed in silence while Modesty twisted the thick chain holding that vulgar, gold cross, and I started to feel slightly more mellow. No stomach pain. No contortions. Only a couple of itches, nudging me, like sand under a wet bikini. Hunches. I welcomed them. I decided that the Chablis had turned out to be fine wine and that I would live. I also decided to make amends to Modesty. And to keep her too busy playing detective to fret over Rickie.

"Okay, here's what we're going to do," I said. "First, we'll speak to Mom and Gypsy Rose, to let them know that you're alive and well and to find out what time I have to be at Edwina's; second, we'll arrange to catch up with Dennis later, I have a few questions for him; then, as soon as Too Tall Tom arrives, we're off to Hell's Kitchen."

"Why are we going there?" Modesty asked.

"I still believe that Holly Halligan and Charlie Fione's deaths are connected to Hell's Kitchen, and if Rickie isn't their killer, I have a hunch about one of the neighbors that might lead us to whodunit!"

During our taxi ride uptown, Too Tall Tom talked from Tribeca to Times Square. "My dears, I wish you could have seen it. Wanda broke down at the bier, crying like she'd lost her best friend and claiming that she had to do a sixth step." When Wanda left me in the ladies' room, she'd been on the fourth step. I guess she'd decided not to take the fifth.

"Jane made a few phone calls and pulled a mini Ghostwriters Anonymous meeting together. Serenity Sue—" Modesty and I groaned. Too Tall Tom rolled right on: "Listen, ladies, any ghost in a gale. Anyway, Jane finally managed to pull Wanda away from the casket and off they went to work on Wanda's defects. But before they got out the door, Ben arrived. Wanda stopped weeping long enough to deliver a tirade to Ben, shouting out all the reasons why Rickie Romero had to be the killer."

Modesty brought her hands up to her face, hiding her expression. Too Tall Tom patted her arm and changed his direction. "However, our man in homicide had another mourner on his mind. He was looking for you, Jake. I told him you'd just left, but I didn't say where you'd gone. It wasn't easy, trying to escape from your mother and Gypsy Rose and get down to Hunter's. And Dennis Kim kept asking leading questions. I gather you left him in the lurch, too. Both Ben and Dennis were moping around Campbell's like teenagers who'd been stood up for the prom. You must stop recycling your men like garbage, Jake. Take it straight from my broken heart, you'll wind up dancing in the dump pile . . . alone!"

Citing Too Tall Tom's sensitivity, the taxi driver, a handsome Pakistani, asked him for a date.

Mrs. Casey not only remembered me, but invited us all up, then turned off *Wheel of Fortune* to answer my questions. "As long as you're out of here before *Jeopardy!*" The old lady's sharp wit, good humor, and warm hospitality seemed to thaw Modesty's icy attitude, sparking her interest and, almost, eliciting a smile.

The apartment, a railroad flat like Carita's, also featured a bathtub in the kitchen, though Mrs. Casey had filled it with ferns. "The late Mr. Casey built a shower in the bathroom, but I fancied the old tub, so I reinvented it as a flowerpot."

Turning down her offer of tea—though none of us had eaten anything since Mom's breakfast, we were running short on time: I had that appointment with Gypsy Rose to talk to Edwina Fione at eight-thirty and we'd agreed to pick up a pizza on our way home—I moved the conversation from memories to murder. "Mrs. Casey, you mentioned that one of the three Houlihan brothers was still alive but serving time in jail. I'd like to talk to him. Could you tell me where he is?"

If the Romeros hadn't exacted revenge—via Rickie— on Charlie Fione, I thought, just maybe the Houlihan family's only surviving brother had used his fellow cons' connections to hire a hit man to execute the senator. And, in a Greek tragedy twist, the woman whose rape was being avenged had died along with her rapist. The writer in me loved this theory. And Modesty bought into it, too, because it exonerated Rickie. Too Tall Tom had reserved judgment—insisting, again, that Maurice Welch was our man—but I'm sure he considered my theory to be science fiction.

With Mrs. Casey's response—"Ah, but Jake, the poor man's been in the prison hospital, in a coma, for over a decade now"—my bright idea entered the twilight zone.

When we were leaving, Too Tall Tom, admiring the moldings, wall panels, and doorknobs as well as Mrs. Casey's 1930s furniture, asked our hostess if he could redecorate but not update—"it's totally charming as is"— her apartment, then use the before-and-after shots in his own work-in-progress, *Old Is New*.

"Let me think about that overnight, young man," Mrs. Casey told him. "At my age, I never take longer than twelve hours to make a decision. Will you be at Senator Fione's funeral at St. Patrick's?"

"No," Too Tall Tom said, sounding somewhat put out, "but Jake will."

"Are you going to the funeral?" I asked Mrs. Casey.

"Mrs. Fione is sending a limousine for me in the morning." The old lady smiled. "I'll give you my deci- sion after Mass; then you can relay it to your friend.

Look for me outside the cathedral. Or will you be aboard the Ashes Away cruise?"

I nodded. "Yes. I'll see you there. Thanks for talking to us."

We marched, single file, down the three flights of stairs. Too Tall Tom, bringing up the rear, asked, "How does Mrs. Casey do this every day? She has to be ninety!"

Modesty said, "Strength of character. That's one feisty lady. How about that Edwina inviting Charlie's old neighbor to attend both his funeral and his final fling? Of course, she might only have done it for the good press that the gesture is bound to generate, or the widow Fione's cold exterior could be covering a generous spirit."

The wind-chill factor smacked me in the face as I came out the front door. Burying my chin into my scarf, I wished I'd thrown a coat over my pantsuit. "It's going to be mighty cold cruising around Manhattan tomorrow."

"Is that you, Jake O'Hara?" a deep voice asked.

Jimmy Roosevelt had one foot on the brownstone's stoop and his right hand extended out in greeting.

I introduced him to Modesty and Too Tall Tom. "This is the man who tackled me in order to save my face from that bucket of red paint. How you doing, Jimmy?"

"Great." He laughed. "I'm on my way up to Mrs. Casey's. We have a dinner date for *Jeopardy!* every Tuesday night. With a fin riding on the Final Jeopardy question. Unfortunately, she usually wins." He waved the bag in his left hand. "My homemade baked ziti. We served it for lunch at work, but Mrs. Casey loves it, so it's encoring for dinner. You'll have to come by and sample it one night, Jake. Bring Modesty and Too Tall

Tom. Funny we should run into each other; I planned on calling you after the show."

"What's up?"

"Well, this may mean nothing," Jimmy said, "but one of the kids in the building just mentioned to me that on the night that the bucket was tossed off the roof, he remembered seeing something strange. This boy lives on the top floor, and as he was about to start down the five flights of stairs, he noticed a leprechaun heading up the stairs to the roof. Since this sighting had occurred right after St. Patty's Day, the kid figured that someone was still partying. But then he got to thinking—"

"A male or female leprechaun?" Modesty asked.

"The kid only got a quick look." Jimmy shrugged. "Slim, he said, wearing a mask and one of those green high hats, you know, with a buckle."

"Oh . . . we know!" I said. "Thanks, Jimmy, and we'll take you up on that invitation for baked ziti."

With his free hand he reached into his jacket pocket and pulled out a business card. "Call me at work. I'm there more than I'm at home." Then he went through the door that Too Tall Tom had continued to hold open.

Glancing at the card, I read: *James Roosevelt, Executive Director, the Romero Foundation for the Homeless, Sacred Heart Parish Hall.*

"Jesus H. Christ!" I yelled, startling a passerby.

"I thought you said his name was Jimmy." Too Tall Tom closed the door.

Twenty-nine

The pizza tasted rubbery. And I decided that I really couldn't stomach diet Coke. I thought about Jimmy Roosevelt. If stranded for life on a desert island, forced to choose the same meal every day for the duration, my choice would be baked ziti, Italian bread, real butter, and Classic Coke—no one would be there to watch me grow fat—and, for dessert, chocolate cream pie and hot tea. About now, isolation and all, that seemed like a good scenario.

Gypsy Rose and Mom hovered over Modesty and me, demanding details, fussing over facts, not one bit happy to be receiving our *Reader's Digest* abridged version. Too Tall Tom had passed on the pizza. I suspected our fickle friend would be dining in the "delightful little Pakistani place in NoHo" that our taxi driver had recommended while emphasizing he'd be having dinner there tonight himself.

Starved, I shoveled in a slice; Gypsy Rose and I had less than thirty minutes till our appointment with Edwina. Swallowing an amazingly long string of cheese, I said, "Can we bring Modesty with us?" I was afraid to let her out of my sight. She might hear from Rickie and vanish, permanently, with him.

"Of course, darling," my mother said. "I plan to tag along, too." I had to chuckle. Clearly, Mom didn't want me out of her sight either. "And Jake, Dennis phoned. He's tied up in some sort of late meeting with Pax Publishing. Sounded stressed, but said that if he's finished before midnight, he'll call you."

Edwina Carrington Fione kept an apartment in the Waldorf Towers. With her late husband, she also owned a condo in the Watergate, a floor above Bob Dole's, and a country house in upstate Putnam County. When we hopped out of the cab on Fiftieth and Park, Mom decided that she absolutely had to use the ladies' room, so we all trooped across the Waldorf-Astoria's square-block lobby to, except for Gypsy Rose's Plaza suite, the number-one john in Manhattan. The detour confirmed Mom's rating; the lighting alone made the trip worthwhile. Haggard at home, I now almost glowed in my private stall's makeup mirror. Giving my mother great satisfaction, I told her to go ahead and install her preferred pink lightbulbs in my bathroom.

As the four of us walked toward the Tower Suites, Modesty spotted Donald Jay stepping out of an elevator. We stopped abruptly and stood, clustered behind a potted palm, trying not to be observed spying. But Jay, far too engrossed in his companion, tête-à-tête with none other than the junior senator from New York, never noticed us.

The same elevator whisked us up into a small, elegant foyer, with velvet walls and high ceilings, that led to Edwina's open door. The widow looked wonderful. Lots

of soft pink lighting in this apartment. "Welcome, ladies," Mrs. Fione's cultured voice greeted us. "Everyone
else has gone home, but I hope you will all join me in
a nightcap. Let's toast Charlie!"

Asking Mom to pour the champagne and Modesty and
me to round up the crystal flutes. Edwina explained that
she needed a moment or two alone with Gypsy Rose.
They went off to the library and I checked out the living
room. Except for the contemporary photographs crowd-
ing the mantel, the tabletops, and the baby grand, we
could have been standing in a nineteenth-century Lon-
don salon.

Prominently displayed on the piano was a recent shot
of Senator Fione and Donald Jay, flanked by Ashley
Butler and Wanda Sparks. Under their trademark high
hairdos, both women wore too much makeup and looks
of awed adoration, directed at Charlie. In a silver frame,
an eleven-by-fourteen glossy, taken in the Oval Office,
was inscribed with words of praise from a former president, who'd posed with his arm draped around the senator. I picked up a photograph of Senator Fione standing
next to his New York colleague, thinking how her sen-
sible short haircut contrasted with Ashley and Wanda's
styles. And in this woman's eyes, I saw neither awe nor
adoration.

"You're staring into the face of the now senior senator
from the state of New York. Charlie's real hell must be
the torture of accepting that ugly bit of destiny." The
widow had returned. "Shall we drink our champagne,
ladies?" Mrs. Fione strode across the room, trailed by
Gypsy Rose, who was moving her hands in quick, little
circles, sending a TV producer's standard signal for
"let's speed it up." I wondered what had transpired in

the library. Did Edwina know that her husband had been a teenage rapist?

We raised our glasses. "To Charlie Fione," my mother said tentatively, wrinkling her nose as if she smelled something foul. I knew that Mom considered her formerly favorite senator to be a fallen idol.

Gypsy Rose bit her lip . . . but remained silent.

"On whatever plane," Edwina's dulcet tones rolled out, "where the low-life bastard is destined to spend eternity!" She chugged down her drink. "I'm praying that the Marquis de Sade has been assigned as Charlie's permanent roommate."

"I'll drink to that!" Modesty said.

The doorman hailed a cab. We all squeezed into the backseat, sensing that secrets were about to be swapped and promises broken. Gypsy Rose went first.

"This morning, right before the viewing, Edwina discovered that her late husband had been having an affair with—surprise!—another mystery writer."

"How?" I asked.

"E-mails!" Gypsy Rose said. Edwina searched through Charlie's computer files—she had his password—and the old fool had saved copies of his electronic love letters. Among her other virtues, like delectable thighs, they salute his mistress's writing style."

"So," my mother said, "is it Wanda, Ashley, or is what we have here one touch of Venus?"

"My thoughts exactly, Maura!" Gypsy Rose said. "You must be psychic, too! The e-mails arrived from cupcake@lovenotes.com; however, when Edwina investigated, Cupcake's on-line service wouldn't disclose the name of the person behind her electronic nickname. I sense that Charlie needed to boast about being in love with another woman, knowing that his wife wouldn't be able to identify the object of his affection. Anyway, Edwina printed out several of his e-mails and they're hot stuff. No question, the senator was smitten. When I channel him tomorrow on the Ashes Away cruise his widow expects Charlie to reveal his lover's name!"

"Drama on the high seas!" I said. "Will that scene be played before or after she flings his ashes?"

"Before," Gypsy Rose said, "and that's not all she'll be tormenting Charlie about! Edwina is seriously considering Donald Jay's suggestion that she complete Fione's term in the Senate."

"Sure," Modesty said. "So Edwina can vote—with her sister witch of a senator—against the environment and for that snake Donald Jay's site."

After all this, could Edwina be the murderer? I had several questions. "How long has Edwina had Charlie's password?"

"Smart girl, Jake," Gypsy Rose said. "From what she said, I gathered that he'd given it to her on St. Patrick's Day. Before the Crime Conference."

"The day he died," Modesty said. "I don't believe that could be just a coincidence, do any of you? I bet she killed him!" Her qualified approval of Edwina had dissipated.

"But even if Edwina had found the e-mails that same morning," I said, "how could she have hired the leprechaun so quickly?"

Modesty looked at me with scorn. "With the Carrington money behind her, one short phone call to Murder, Inc. would have resolved that problem for Edwina. Goddamn it, Jake, sometimes, you're so smart, you're lame. And thick! Your relentless inquisition drove Rickie to jump off my balcony!"

"What!" My mother screamed as the taxi came to a screeching halt in front of Mr. Kim's fruit stand.

Once we were back in our kitchen, with Mom pouring tea and Gypsy Rose slicing lemon pound cake, I decided to lay everything out on the table. Omitting only my feelings of fear, I related the unsettling and puzzling events of my long day. The tale ended with my summation, citing reasonable doubt about Rickie's guilt, and its telling managed to lift up the dam that had been holding back Modesty's emotions. She actually hugged me.

"He's the only man I've ever cared about," Modesty said, with more passion than I would have believed her to be capable of. "Jake, you have to help me clear Rickie!"

"Where is he now?" I asked. My mother, frowning, perched on the edge of her chair, teacup poised in mid-air. Gypsy Rose, leaning in closer to Modesty, wiped away a tear. They were loving this, no doubt, reveling in being part of the action and sharing in Modesty's and my confidences while chomping at the bit to contribute to the resolution of this star-crossed love story.

Modesty hesitated, then sighed and looked around the table, meeting each of our eyes. "I'm going to trust you." For a misogynist, this had to be a major breakthrough. Blinking, I fought off my own tears. "Rickie has returned to my apartment. He dropped onto the balcony below mine; then, when you and the doorman left—Rickie watched you walk to the corner, Jake—he hoisted himself back up. You hadn't locked the glass door. After Hunter called me at Campbell's, I rang home, using the signal that Rickie and I had devised, and he told me about your visit. However, I couldn't go home. First, I had to find out what Hunter wanted, then I didn't want you to get suspicious, so I ran around town playing Dr.

Watson. Now I hope that you ladies have gathered enough information to come up with whodunit, but I'm going home to spend the night with Rickie. It may be our last."

As Modesty left, secure in the knowledge that romance had won over reason and accepting our promises to keep her secret till tomorrow morning, while assuring us that Rickie wouldn't bolt before then, Mom buzzed Dennis up and the phone rang. A hell of a lot of activity for almost eleven o'clock at the end of what, by anyone's standard, had been a damn busy day!

The call was for Mom. Aaron. And where might his son be? I heard my mother say, "The governor?" Though very curious, I stopped eavesdropping to let Dennis in, remembering that I'd been the one who wanted to talk to him. Gypsy Rose said hello, then excused herself to do the dishes, and I led Dennis into the living room. Mom must have taken the portable phone into her bedroom.

"What can I do for you?" he asked. I wondered if he had any idea that the glint in his great eyes ignited my heart. I stared at him in silence. "Come on, Jake. Tell me. I want to go to bed; I should have phoned, but I wanted to see you—er—to make sure that you're okay."

For a second, totally brain-dead, I forgot what I'd wanted to know. Something about . . . Ashley Butler . . . oh . . . I had a sudden flash of memory. "When Ashley stopped by here, on Monday, to ask me to ghost for her, she said that Charlie Fione had recommended her to Pax Publishing. Did she have a special relationship with the senator? It struck me as odd at the time. Then tonight, Edwina told Gypsy Rose that the senator had been indiscreet, having an affair with another mystery writer—"

"Strange, how timing is everything." Dennis smiled.

"During my otherwise tedious meeting with the management of Pax, Fione's editor did drop two tidbits that caught my attention. You know that Maurice Welch ghosted *Death of a Filibuster*." I nodded. "Welch is in such a rage over the senator promising, but not paying, those big bucks that now he wants to sue Pax as well as Fione's estate."

"And the second tidbit?"

"The senator had given Pax's legal department specific instructions that all his royalties—Welch's money was to have come out of the advance—should go directly to Miss Ashley Butler."

"Jesus!" Exhausted, I rested my head against the back of the couch. Suddenly Dennis's eyes came closer to mine, then his lips gently kissed me. I flung my arms around him, hanging on as if my life depended on it. He whispered in my ear, "Jake, is it our turn? I do love you, you know. I guess I always have."

God knows what would have happened next if loud laughter hadn't preceded my mother and Gypsy Rose's entrance into the room.

"Boy, will Edwina be annoyed," my mother was saying. "There's going to be a special election to fill Charlie Fione's seat."

"He's not even in his grave yet," I said. "Right now I'm more interested in who killed Charlie Fione than in who will replace him in the Senate."

"But, Jake," Mom said, "the governor just called Aaron and asked him to run. Your mother may become a Washington wife!"

Thirty

The sun couldn't have shone more brightly this morning if I'd been in St. Croix, dashing for a dip in the ocean, instead of in Carnegie Hill, dressing for a funeral at St. Patrick's.

I'd spent a night filled with bizarre dreams, mixed emotions, and a rude awakening. The dreams were about Mom, suddenly, turning into this century's Perle Mesta, charming D.C. society, leaving me struggling alone in Manhattan. The emotions ran the gamut from guilt to lust. If I cared so deeply about Ben Rubin, how come I so desperately wanted to bed Dennis Kim? And finally, the awakening, better rude than never, might be considered a psychological thunderbolt. Sometime in the night I'd been hit over the head with whodunit!

Sneaking into the kitchen, trying not to wake Mom, I boiled water for tea and toasted a bagel, wanting to sate myself while rehearsing my lines, before calling Edwina. When the clock struck eight, I dialed her number.

"This is Edwina Carrington Fione." She and her perfect vowels sounded tired.

"Jake O'Hara, Mrs. Fione. Sorry to bother you, today of all days, but I need to ask you something very important."

"I'm listening."

I had to be cagey here; I didn't want her to suspect that Gypsy Rose had told us all about Edwina having searched through Charlie's electronic mail. "Would you know if the senator had any correspondence with Holly Halligan shortly before they were murdered? Maybe letters? Phone messages? Or e-mail?"

"No letters. At least not here in New York. There could be some letters from Miss Halligan in the senator's office in Washington, but his chief of staff hasn't mentioned any." She sighed. "I'd forgotten about this, Miss O'Hara, but now that you mention it, there was a message on the answering machine the day before Charlie died. From Holly Halligan."

"What did it say?"

"Nothing much. Just that Charlie should call her, and I quote, 'Like yesterday!' Since they'd both been scheduled to appear on the same Crime Writers' Conference panel the next day, I naturally assumed Holly Halligan wanted to talk to him about that. I gave my husband her message."

"And?"

"And I presume he returned her call. Where in the world are you going with this, Miss O'Hara?"

"Please indulge me, Mrs. Fione. Is there any way you could check to see if there was any e-mail exchanged between Holly and your husband?"

"Well, I am trying to get ready to escort the senator's remains from Campbell's to the cathedral. I'm meeting

Father Fione and Charlie's sister, Fatima Fione-Epstein, the governor, and a congressional delegation at the funeral parlor—"

"It's really urgent!"

"All right. But I may not have time to call you back. If there is any e-mail, I'll print it out and bring it with me." She hung up.

Mom appeared wearing Velcro rollers and a clay mask. I poured her tea, then retreated to my bedroom to call Ben. Aaron, my future stepfather and, as the governor's handpicked candidate, probably New York's future senator, answered on the first ring. "Ben's not here, Jake. He's on his way downtown. Rickie Romero showed up at the Nineteenth, a few minutes ago, with his attorney in tow."

Pleased that Rickie had lived up to Modesty's expectations but disappointed that once again I couldn't connect with Ben, I hesitated.

"Hey, Jake, don't hang up. Ben said to tell you that he'll see you at the funeral and that he misses you."

"Yeah. Well, Aaron, I have a message for him, too. Tell Ben that he's booking the wrong man—and I'd suggest he check out Charlie Fione's e-mail."

Then I called Modesty and hopped into in the shower, before realizing that I'd never congratulated Aaron.

. . . . .

We were seated in a row toward the left rear of St. Patrick's, near the statue of St. John Neumann. A relatively recent addition, this modern, alabaster, somewhat stark statue differed, dramatically, from the more traditional renditions of the longer canonized, whose statues were ensconced in their own niches, circling the cathedral. Today, as usual, the large array

of vigil candles found in front of these saints blazed
brightly.

The Crime Writers filled the pew. The lineup, starting
from the center aisle, was Donald Jay, Wanda Sparks,
Ashley Butler, Venus DeMill, Maurice Welch, Hunter
Greene, then Mom, Gypsy Rose, and Modesty, with me
on the far side, closest to the confessional, St. John, and
the candles.

Modesty, mourning neither Holly Halligan's nor
Charlie Fione's death, but rather Rickie Romero's
decision to turn himself in, knelt in prayer. A pious mini-
monk, in her brown habitlike long dress and gold cross.
When we picked her up in the taxi, she'd greeted me
with an order. "Find the killer before we disembark from
this Ashes Away cruise, Jake, or else Rickie will sail
straight onto death row." Then, indicating her high level
of distress, she allowed my mother to hold her hand all
the way down Fifth Avenue to St. Patrick's. Now, as
she fiddled with her rosary belt, I watched that hand
tremble. If my middle-of-the-night thunderbolt had been
on   target,   I   would—happily—honor   and   obey
Modesty's command.

As the three tenors, accompanied by the organist and
a string quartet, filled the cathedral with the moving
refrain of "Ave Maria," Venus wept like a woman who'd
lost her one true love. I felt certain that she cried for
Carita, not Charlie. The torrent of tears gushing from
Wanda and Ashley confused me. Why, if Ashley was,
as I suspected, a.k.a. cupcake@lovenotes.com, would
Wanda be wailing like a banshee? To further complicate
my theory, I spotted Dr. Nujurian, two pews in front of
ours, slouched and seemingly suffering from such grief
that her perky persona had morphed into a head-to-toe,
black-and-white portrait of inconsolable misery. Even

her pillbox hat had fallen forward onto her her forehead. Would, by some sick twist of fate, Dr. Assisted Suicide turn out to be both a mystery writer and Charlie's cupcake? What could have driven each of these women to reach heights of sadness that defied rationality? Especially since the senator's widow had walked down the aisle appearing as cool as a chunk of dry ice.

Midway through the senator's second eulogy, I dozed off. My daydream was worse than any nightmare. I found myself back in the Grand Ballroom of the Plaza, dressed as a leprechaun, serving a pitcher of green beer. Rickie Romero laughed as the two poisoned panelists, their faces contorted in pain, rose up from the floor. A dead Holly Halligan sang a sorrowful "Danny Boy." I tried to run, but my legs wouldn't move. The corpse of Charlie Fione stretched a long arm toward me, grabbing my hair, pulling me close to him, and whispering in my ear, "Let me rest in peace!" A swell of organ music jerked me awake. I stifled a scream, startling my mother.

In the center aisle, the cardinal and the altar boys circled the senator's golden urn, the smell of incense wafted through the cathedral, and from the altar Father Fione led the faithful in the Roman Catholic Church's centuries-old prayer for the dead. "May his soul and all the souls of the faithful departed rest in peace."

Thirty-one

The long line of black limousines stretched up Fifth Avenue from St. Patrick's to the Pierre Hotel. The funeral directors, moving rather frantically, separated those mourners who would be going aboard the Ashes Away cruise from the more fortunate and much larger group who now were free to go on with their own lives. Edwina Carrington Fione, still an ice matron, emerged from the cathedral with the governor, who escorted her to the lead limo. Charlie Fione's urn was nowhere in sight.

Mrs. Casey, wearing black and looking like the subject of a 1950s Norman Rockwell painting, exited on the arm of the mayor, reveling in his undivided attention. Each time I concluded that the widow Fione was a total creep, another example of her devotion to detail or her concern for people would astound me. I waved and the old lady winked at me. "Isn't this one grand funeral, Jake?"

Modesty, Gypsy Rose, Mom, and I had been assigned to car number seven, but as its driver pulled up in front of the cathedral, Dennis Kim arrived, brakes screeching, and double-parked his Rolls-Royce—its top was down—alongside the last of three open and overflowing flower cars. "Jake, your chariot awaits!" he yelled across the gladiolas.

We were embarking from a Chelsea pier, where an almost carnival atmosphere prevailed. At noon, the sun had warmed the city and the cloudless sky was baby blue. The Hudson River seemed to sparkle in the sunshine. And on its west bank, even New Jersey appeared picture perfect.

Venus DeMill climbed up the gangplank behind me. "An Ashes Away cruise can cost more than a first-class crossing on the *Queen Mary*," she said. I turned and smiled, nodding. She wrapped an arm around Maurice Welch's thick waist. "After we've tucked our poor, darling Carita into the ground for her long sleep, we'll be honeymooning on the *Queen*. Sailing as soon as Maurice collects his refund from Holly Halligan's estate and his money for ghosting that deadbeat Charlie Fione's book, from Pax Publishing. For sure, Edwina isn't going to ante up."

"My dear," Maurice said, "Jake doesn't need to hear all this. We've come to bury Charlie not berate him."

Ignoring her fiancé, Venus pointed her index finger at Dr. Nujurian, who'd just stepped out of limousine number four, followed by Ashley Butler and Wanda Sparks. "That's the bitch who, at Holly's command, killed on commission. But never again! I just heard on the limo's radio that the doctor's license to practice has been revoked by the state of New York. No wonder she was crying."

The Ashes Away company's captain, in a Gilbert and Sullivan full-dress uniform, reached out for my hand and I climbed aboard. The *Valhalla* was some ship. An im-

maculate white wooden character boat, circa the 1920s,
designed and built when the rich really were different
from you and me. Dennis took us on the grand tour.
Magnificently maintained, the seventy-five foot-long
craft featured gleaming mahogany decks, brass railings,
and highly polished steps, leading to beautifully ap-
pointed salons and cabins. But not an inch of fiberglass.
She also had four heads and, while smaller, each was as
impressive as the Waldorf-Astoria's ladies' room!

As Modesty, Mom, Gypsy Rose, and I followed Dennis down to the posh grand salon, a piano player greeted
us with a medley of New York songs. A candlelit buffet
table, spanning the width of the ship, had been laid with
fine linen, sterling silver, bone china, and covered with
gourmet food that had been supplied from the River
Café. According to our carefully charted itinerary, we
would be disembarking at that same restaurant's dock
after having cruised around the Battery, then flinging
Charlie's ashes overboard before we sailed under the
Brooklyn Bridge.

But, at the moment, what remained of Senator Charlie
Fione could be viewed in the petite salon. The golden
urn stood alone, centered on a small, carved table that
had been placed in front of heavy, maroon velvet drapes,
shutting out any sunlight. Tall baskets of lilies flanked
either side of the oak table, as did three pairs of equally
tall candles, their flickering lights providing the salon's
only illumination. Bamboo and cane folding chairs, arranged in neat rows, indicated that Edwina might be
planning on a formal good-bye prior to her late husband's final fling. The eleven-by-fourteen photograph of
the dead senator and the former president that I'd seen
in Edwina's Waldorf Towers apartment had been
propped up in front of one of the draped portholes.

Suddenly I felt sick. My mother, speaking for all of us, said, "Let's get out of here!"

We returned on deck, where I gulped the clean, fresh spring air and watched our fellow passengers board.

Would this Ashes Away cruise upset Hunter Green? Certainly, it would have to bring back bad memories of his wife's final voyage. He was coming aboard now, along with Wanda Sparks. Deep in conversation. His arm around her shoulder. Well, he had been her mentor, introducing her to Rickie Romero and brokering her ghostwriting assignment. I suppose they still could be close friends. Yet . . .

"Why, Dennis Kim!" Ashley Butler's honey-sugared-ham accent jarred me. "How surprised and de . . . light . . . ed I am to see you! I've been dreading *mal de mer* and worried about this old vessel sinking, but with a gentleman like you aboard, I do feel ever so much safer."

Modesty twisted her chain into a knot. Her obscene gold cross stuck straight out and poked Ashley in her left breast. "And I do hope that you can swim." She mimicked Ashley's drawl. "This yacht is yar, but she has no lifeboats."

Dr. Nujurian emerged from below. "Isn't this just a super day for a burial at sea?" she asked of no one in particular while standing at the starboard deck rail and staring out across the Hudson. "Death can be such an uplifting experience."

"You really should experience it firsthand," Modesty told her. The doctor spun around, then recognizing Modesty and me, scurried back down to the salon.

Some stragglers, including several senators and Donald Jay, embarked. The captain called Mrs. Fione over to review the passenger roster. Putting on gold-framed reading glasses, she scanned the list and announced, "Thirty-six. I think that's everyone."

"Hoist anchor!" the captain ordered the first mate.

The crew released the lines and I thought: Ben missed the boat.

Thirty-two

The *Valhalla* slowly cruised down the Hudson as her passengers milled about, looking uncomfortable. Most of the Washington contingent had gravitated to the well-stocked bar, located in an alcove in the main salon and manned by an efficient young bartender dressed in a navy blazer. Martinis seemed to be the Ashes Away crowd's drink of choice. Gypsy Rose had decided to "try and eat a little something; that's quite a buffet." And Mom, agreeing—"it would be a sin to waste all that shrimp"—joined her. Then Modesty had gone off to "have a word" with Hunter.

Snatches of conversation rose through the salon's open hatch—which looked more like a small skylight—to where Dennis and I stood portside, watching the city slip by. We'd passed Battery Park and were approaching Wall Street. Mrs. Casey was talking to Dr. Fatima Fione-Epstein and her loud, gravelly voice carried well. "Fatima, the reason that the Irish and the Italians don't commit suicide isn't religious. It's not their Catholic faith. It's their diet. Potatoes and pasta. Starch contains an antidote to depression, you know." Dr. Fione-Epstein's response was lost in a waterfront church's chimes.

"That's an interesting theory," I said to Dennis, "but not one that I could agree with. Have you met Mrs. Casey yet?"

"No, but I'm looking forward to it." He smoothed my windblown hair.

"Dennis, while we have a moment alone here, I need to tell you something."

"Well, right now we aren't ships just passing in the night, are we?" Dennis kissed my forehead, then smiled. "We're on the same deck, but I'd hoped for a more romantic occasion then a cremation cruise to discuss our future."

"I don't want to talk about us," I said. His glorious, gold-flecked eyes clouded. "I mean I do, but not here, not now." I reached up, cupped his face in my hands, and kissed him. Deeply.

"Soon?" He pulled me closer. "Is that a promise?" He kissed me again. Madly.

I came up for breath. "Truly, Dennis, that's a promise."

"Okay, what else is on your mind?"

The World Trade Center loomed dead ahead of us. "I'm not sure if I can prove all this, but I know who poisoned the panel and I know who killed Carita and I think I even know why."

"And a lot of knowledge is a dangerous thing!" Wanda Sparks announced, coming up behind us from the stern. I wondered how much of our conversation she'd overheard. "Modesty is back there, quizzing Hunter as if she *knows* that he's the killer. And he's innocent, of course. Jake, you would do well to remember that what we perceive to be the truth often isn't. Your Ghost-writers Anonymous program taught me that!"

"Hunter Green has an airtight alibi for Carita Magenta's murder," I said. "Modesty knows—er, has been told that."

"Yes," Wanda said. "But I don't." She gripped the railing. "Your friend is so besotted with Rickie Romero that she's convinced herself that Hunter had *me* kill Carita in order to retrieve the Faith diamond. Such insanity!" She laughed. "As if I would have drowned Carita before she'd eaten her lasagna."

"Maybe not so insane," I said, thinking my thunderbolt had fizzled. "How do you know about that full plate of lasagna, Wanda? It wasn't mentioned in the papers or on TV. Rickie told Hunter; that's how I know. But I don't think Hunter—or Venus—would have told you. Jesus, you were there, weren't you?"

Though I couldn't fathom how she had another tear left to squeeze out, Wanda resumed her god-awful weeping. "I can't seem to stop crying. I'm so scared. Jake, I swear I didn't kill Carita. The apartment door was open. Her head was in that old purple tub; her big butt sticking up out of it. I panicked and ran back down those stairs fast as I could! I just wanted to help Hunter; he doesn't even know I was there. Rickie betrayed my love, but Hunter's been so good to me and—"

"Wanda, tell me, what were you doing at Carita's?"

"Looking for the Faith diamond. Hunter wasn't the only one who figured out where Rickie had stashed it." She shook her head. "I wanted Hunter to have it. That bastard Rickie had no right to it, did he?"

Dennis chuckled. "Well, strange as it might sound for me to bring up ethics, from a legal—or any other—point of view, that diamond is still stolen property and not yours to give to anyone."

I wasn't done with Wanda. "When you arrived, Carita was already dead. Did you see anyone else? This is important."

She hung her head. "Yes. As I was leaving, Rickie was turning the corner; I don't think he saw me."

"Or maybe he did, but didn't say anything in order to protect you!" I said as the *Valhalla* rounded the tip of Manhattan Island. "So Carita Magenta had been murdered well before Romero appeared on the scene? Wanda, you can be a witness in his defense!"

"Jake! Come down here!" my mother screamed through the hatch.

Confusion reigned in the grand salon. Senators, Crime Writers, and the Fione siblings were cowering by the buffet table and the bar while Ashley Butler and Edwina Carrington Fione struggled in the center of the salon, engaged in a tug-of-war over Charlie Fione's urn.

"He's mine!" Ashley shouted. "I did what he wanted. Now I deserve to spend eternity with him!"

"What happened?" I asked my mother.

"Gypsy Rose was ready to begin channeling. Actually, we think Charlie Fione may be on his way here from the world beyond. The mourners were about to take their seats in the small salon when Ashley suddenly grabbed the urn. Edwina intercepted her before she could climb on deck. I gather Ashley wants to fling herself into the river along with Charlie!"

Dennis moved so quickly, retrieving the urn from the women's clutches, I don't think that, at first, either of them realized what had happened. Then Ashley kicked Dennis in the groin and he dropped the urn. Ashley swooped down, picked it up, and ran into the petite salon. On her heels, I tripped and stumbled, giving Ashley a chance to latch the door behind us.

"No one can stop me from spending eternity with my charming Charlie!" Ashley cried. Her high hair had collapsed along with her features.

"Your charming Charlie murdered Holly Halligan," I told her, "then committed suicide, and not knowing that Romero didn't drink, the senator died believing he'd killed Rickie, too. And Cupcake, you dressed up as leprechaun to help him."

"I had no idea that Charlie planned on taking Holly and Rickie with him! When Romero found Holly Halligan and they threatened to ruin the senator's reputation, right there at the Plaza, in front of his wife and his fellow Crime Writers, Charlie begged me to help him kill himself. He was dying of cancer, anyway. So, yes, I served the poisoned beer. And I'd do it again to protect my Charlie!"

"To protect Charlie. That's why you tried to frame Carita Magenta, isn't it? Dropping the bucket of red paint on me? Mailing those red-crayon threats to Dr. Nujurian? And if the police thought Hunter was the killer, that would have been okay with you, too. Just so long as Senator Fione's reputation was protected. And it almost worked. We were all looking for a killer who had a motive for murdering all three panelists and who had no idea that Charlie was already a dead man." I played my hunch. "Magenta knew you were the leprechaun, didn't she?"

"That fat cow Carita spotted me stuffing the costume into the Modess machine. The bitch actually tried to blackmail me!" Ashley lifted one of the tall candles off its stand. "You were such a snoop, Jake, I planned on killing you, too." She swung the candle toward the velvet drapes. They burst into flames, and she smiled. "Now you and this entire ship of fools will burn, along with Charlie and me!" She threw a second candle across the room. I watched, in horror, as the photograph of the senator and the president caught on fire.

She reached for another candle. I somehow managed to unlatch the door, then jerk it open and roll into the grand salon, screaming, "Fire! Watch out!" before the third candle came hurtling through behind me.

That candle landed on the buffet table and the centerpiece went up in flames. Dennis, Maurice, and two of the senators tried to beat out the fire with their jackets, but it quickly spread from the tablecloth to a satin chair. Then, as one of the candles on the buffet table tumbled over onto the floor, igniting a small fringed rug, Ashley stepped into the grand salon, tossing a fourth candle onto a sofa.

The fire now raged in the petite salon. I slammed that door shut and Ashley, still clutching the urn, crawled into a corner of the large room.

The exodus had started. Mom was helping Mrs. Casey, still holding on to her martini, to negotiate the steps up the deck. An unruly line had formed behind them. "Jake!" my mother called. She turned to the man behind her. "Stop pushing! I won't go without my daughter!" The senator from New Jersey placed his hands on Mom's butt and shoved her up and out onto the deck.

As the flames swelled, I realized there wouldn't be enough time for all of us to escape through that exit.

Seeming to concur with my assessment and trying to squeeze in line ahead of the newly senior senator from New York, Dr. Nujurian howled, "I don't want to die. Let me out of here."

Hunter's handsome face appeared in the hatch. "Dennis! Modesty and I can haul some of you up this way. Get them to stand on a chair and have them grab hold of this!" He attached the top of a rope ladder to a cleat and dropped the rest of it down the hatch.

Gypsy Rose and Edwina organized a water brigade, filling ice buckets and bowls with tap water from the sink behind the bar, then passing them to a relay team, composed of the Fione siblings, two senators, and the bartender, who then emptied them on the flames. Based on the heat and smoke levels, I feared they were losing the battle.

I found my purse, pulled out my phone, and called 911. The senator from New York, who had not relinquished her place in the exit line, was already on her cell phone, alerting the coast guard.

Donald Jay smashed open a porthole and stuck his head through it, yelling, "Help! Somebody save us!"

Dennis held the chair steady as Venus kicked off her heels and, with Maurice steadying her, stepped onto the first rung of the narrow ladder.

Hunter grabbed Venus under the arms and, with Modesty's help, hoisted her through the hatch. "You're next, Jake!" Dennis yelled.

"I'm next!" Dr. Nujurian was wild-eyed. She scrambled up on the chair, then stood, using Dennis's head for leverage.

Since the doctor was a much smaller woman than Venus, Hunter had her on deck in no time. I looked around the salon. Less than three left on the line to go up the steps, but the fire was closing in on them. Fatima Fione-Epstein had just exited. Father Fione was right behind her. "Gypsy Rose! Edwina!" I screamed. "Get over here, right now!" Then I reached over and yanked Ashely out of her corner.

Gypsy Rose proved the most agile of all. She gripped the sides of the hatch and helped hoist herself through. As Hunter reached for Edwina, she turned to me. "Jake, there was an odd e-mail from Holly, but my bag, with the printout in it, just burned along with that satin chair!" Ashley pulled away from me and retreated toward the fire.

Dennis said, "I'll drag her up the steps with me. Climb on the chair, Jake. Now!"

The buffet table collapsed and flames lapped against the legs of the chair that I stood on. How the hell would Dennis and Maurice get out? Tears as hot as the flames ran down my cheeks. I stretched my arms through the hatch. I lost my balance and the rope ladder twisted away, leaving my bare feet dangling above the fire as Hunter gripped my armpits. Once on deck, Modesty pushed me. "Jake, run toward the bow! The fire has spread to the stern. We have to jump!" I turned, trying to look back down the hatch, hoping to see Dennis, but all I could see was black smoke and orange flames.

Running forward, we passed Edwina Fione securing a life jacket on Mrs. Casey. "You two okay?" I shouted.

"Isn't this thrilling?" Mrs. Casey said. "We're going to jump!"

My mother and Gypsy Rose, perched on the bow like DiCaprio and Winslet, were waiting for us.

What a view they had! The Statue of Liberty was on our starboard side and the White Hall Terminal on the port side. The Staten Island Ferry was dead ahead. If the captain didn't soon swing to starboard, we could collide. As that thought formed, we veered sharply to the right, Mom and Gypsy Rose fell into the river, and I—think-

ing that I could finally kiss my far-too-often-worn-to-
wakes-and-funerals, DKNY black dress good-bye—
grabbed Modesty's hand and jumped in after them.

Sunshine or not, this water was freezing. Jesus! Had
Dennis and Maurice made it?

Modesty's chain had caught on a starboard line and
she floundered, trying to free it. I swam over, the weight
of my dress seriously cramping my breaststroke style,
and yanked the chain over her head. The clasp opened,
and as the current carried us away from the ship, we
watched her hideous, heavy gold cross sink.

"Well, there goes the Faith diamond, heading straight
down to Davy Jones's locker." Modesty laughed. "I
guess Rickie will be taking up deep-sea diving!"

From the *Valhalla*'s deck, someone bellowed, "Ashes
away!" We looked up and watched Ashley fling Charlie's urn into the water—it missed Modesty's head by
inches—then dive in after it.

Lifeboats were being lowered from the ferry and a
coastguard cutter was approaching. Though I couldn't
see her, I heard my mother shout, "There they are!"

Then Ben called from the cutter, "Jake!" And, suddenly, they were close enough for me to see his face
light up.

Mom, Gypsy Rose, Edwina, and Mrs. Casey were already on board. Strong arms pulled Modesty, me, and a
kicking and screaming Ashley into the boat.

Ben hugged me. "I thought I lost you!" Over his
shoulder, I spotted Dennis and Maurice, their faces covered in soot, swimming toward us. Dennis's warm smile
tickled my cold toes.

ACKNOWLEDGMENTS

A special thank you to Etta Kavanagh, for great editing and grace, under the pressure of my deadline.

As always, my deep appreciation goes to Joyce Sweeney, my mentor, for her insight and critique of the manuscript. For listening to those ever-changing plot twists, my thanks to Doris Holland, Susan Kavanagh, Aline Martinez and Gloria Rothstein.

Thanks to my son, Bill Reckdenwald, whose company works with cruise lines, for researching the waterfront and answering my geography questions.

Finally, a big thank you to Betty MacCloskey, my neighbor and friend, who came up with the name Ashes Away.